April's words chilled Ali. If the killer had been some-where nearby when the crash occurred, then he was probably still there when the emergency vehicles were dispatched to the scene as well—at the same time Ali herself was driving past on the freeway. That meant they'd come after Ali—with a vengeance.

As someone with the three necessary ingredients—motive, opportunity, and an unidentified accomplice—Ali would be exactly what the detectives wanted and needed, a prime suspect.

RAVE REVIEWS FOR THE FICTION OF NEW YORK TIMES AND USA TODAY BESTSELLING AUTHOR J.A. JANCE

"Jance delivers a devilish page-turner."
—*People*

"Heart-stopping. . . . Jance deftly brings the desert, peo-ple, and towns of Southeastern Arizona to life."
—*Publishers Weekly*

"An intriguing plot, colorful characters."
—*San Diego Union-Tribune*

"Characters so real you want to reach out and hug—or strangle—them. Her dialogue always rings true."
—*Cleveland Plain Dealer*

This title is also available as an eBook

WEB OF EVIL

J.A. JANCE

{ a novel of suspense }

POCKET STAR BOOKS
NEW YORK LONDON TOKYO SYDNEY

The sale of this book without its cover is unauthorized. If you purchased this book without a cover, you should be aware that it was reported to the publisher as "unsold and destroyed." Neither the author nor the publisher has received payment for the sale of this "stripped book."

Pocket Star Books
A Division of Simon & Schuster, Inc.
1230 Avenue of the Americas
New York, NY 10020

This book is a work of fiction. Names, characters, places, and incidents either are products of the author's imagination or are used fictitiously. Any resemblance to actual events or locales or persons, living or dead, is entirely coincidental.

Copyright © 2007 by J.A. Jance

All rights reserved, including the right to reproduce this book or portions thereof in any form whatsoever. For information address Touchstone Subsidiary Rights Deparment, 1230 Avenue of the Americas, New York, NY 10020

First Pocket Star Books paperback edition December 2007

POCKET STAR and colophon are registered trademarks of Simon & Schuster, Inc.

For information about special discounts for bulk purchases, please contact Simon & Schuster Special Sales at 1-800-456-6798 or business@simonandschuster.com.

Manufactured in the United States of America

10 9 8 7 6 5

ISBN-13: 978-1-4165-3773-1
ISBN-10:   1-4165-3773-2

For Donna A., the last missing piece of my childhood.
I've been looking for you for years.

{ PROLOGUE }

When the man opened his eyes, it was so dark that at first he thought they were still closed. So he tried again, but nothing changed. It was dark—a hot, black, stifling darkness that seemed to suck the breath out of him. He sensed movement, heard the whine of tires on pavement, but he had no idea where he was or how he'd gotten there. He tried to move his legs but couldn't. They were jammed up under his belly in a space that was far too small, and they seemed to be tied together somehow.

His hands were stuck behind him, shoved up against something hard. After several minutes of struggling he was finally able to shift his body enough to free them. He was stunned to discover that they, too, had been bound together in the same manner his legs were. The combination of their being tied too tight and being stuck under his body had cut off the circulation. At first his hands were nothing more than a pair of useless and inextricably connected deadweight cudgels. After a few moments the blood returned to his fingers in a rush of needle-and-pin agony.

As his senses gradually reasserted themselves, he realized that the rough surface under his cheek was carpet of some kind, and from somewhere nearby came the distinctive smell of new rubber—a spare tire. That meant he was in the trunk of someone's vehicle being taken God knows where. He tried to shout, but of course he couldn't do that, either. His mouth was taped shut. All that emerged from his throat was a guttural groan.

What was it you were you supposed to do if you found yourself trapped in a vehicle like that? Kick out the taillights, hang an arm out the hole, and signal for help? But he couldn't kick anything. He couldn't move his legs, and his bound hands were still useless.

As the man gradually understood the seriousness of his predicament, his heart beat faster while his breath quickened to short panicky gasps. For a while he was afraid he was going to pass out again, but he fought it—fought to bring his breathing back under control. Fought to concentrate. What the hell was happening? Where was he? Who was doing this? And why?

He tried to remember something about what had gone on before. He had a dim recollection of something like a party. Lots of lights and laughter, lots of girls, lots of liquor. So had he gotten drunk and pissed someone off? Was that what was going on? He knew that given enough scotch he wasn't anyone's idea of Mr. Congeniality, but still . . .

Sweat trickled down the side of his face and dribbled into one eye, burning like fire. Without the use of his hands, there was no way to brush it away.

The vehicle slowed suddenly and swerved to the right, rolling him back onto his hands. Outside he heard the roar of a semi going past followed immediately by another and another. So they were on a busy freeway somewhere—or had just left one. But where? As hot as it was, it had to be somewhere over the mountains—somewhere in the desert. Palm Springs, maybe? Or maybe farther north, up toward Needles and Parker.

Why can't I remember where I was or what happened? he wondered. He had always prided himself on being able to hold his liquor. He wasn't like some of the guys he knew, high-powered wheeler-dealers who would have to call around after a wild night on the town, checking with valets at local watering holes to see where they had left their favorite Porsche or Ferrari. He usually knew exactly where he'd been. He also knew when he'd had enough. But now, his mind was fuzzy. He couldn't quite pull things together—not just tonight, but what had gone on in the days before that, either.

The vehicle slowed again. He braced himself, expecting another right-hand turn. Instead, the vehicle turned sharply to the left and bounced off the pavement and onto a much rougher surface. Fine dust swirled inside the small space, filling his eyes and nostrils, making his eyes water and his nose run. Definitely the desert somewhere.

There was another hard jolting bump, then the vehicle came to a sudden halt. What must have been the driver's door opened and shut. And then there was nothing. No sound at all. At first he hoped and dreaded that the trunk lid would click open and his captor would free him, but that didn't happen. He strained his ears, hoping to establish if the freeway was still near enough that he'd be able to hear semis speeding past, but for the longest time, he heard nothing at all. He felt only the oppressive heat and wondered how long it would be before the oxygen ran out and he suffocated.

He felt it first. The car trembled as if it were alive, as if it were being racked by a bad case of the chills. Then he heard it—a distant rumble growing louder and louder until it turned into an unmistakable roar. The car rocked in concert with the sound until the terrible roar and the shaking were one. It was then the man heard the shrill, earth-shattering screech of a fast-approaching freight train. The whistle sounded once, in a single, long, warning wail. Only then did he realize that whoever had locked him in the trunk had left him on the train tracks—left him there to die.

He struggled desperately against his restraints, but it was no use. He couldn't free himself. The engine of the speeding eastbound train plowed into the stationary vehicle, peeling it open like an empty tin can and then dragging the wreckage along underneath the engine for the additional mile it took for the shaken engineer to finally bring the fully loaded train to a stop. As the engineer spoke to the 911 operator in Palm Springs, he reported having seen something fly up and out of the shattered vehicle, something that had looked more like a rag doll than it did a human being.

{ CHAPTER 1 }

CUTLOOSEBLOG.COM
Thursday, September 15, 2005

For all you cutloose fans out there who've been following my story from the beginning, tomorrow is the day the D-I-V-O-R-C-E becomes final. For those of you who may be new to the site, the last few months have been a bit of a bumpy ride since both my husband and my former employer simultaneously sent me packing in hopes of landing a younger model.

My soon-to-be-ex, aka Fang, as he's known in the blogosphere, called me yesterday. It was the first time I'd heard from him directly in several months. What surprised me more than anything was how much I DIDN'T feel when I heard his voice. That, I believe, is a good sign. It turns out Fang was calling, in his own imperious way, to make sure I'd be in court tomorrow so the divorce decree can be finalized. I could have given him grief about it. Could have claimed I was sick or maimed or just too annoyed to bother driving eight hours plus from Sedona over to L.A. And, had I done so, it would have sent him up a wall. You see, Fang needs this divorce right about now a whole lot more than I do. Our court appearance is scheduled for Friday. Saturday is Fang's wedding day.

I've heard rumors that he and his blushing bride, aka Twink, are planning a big-deal celebration, a catered affair with all the right people in attendance at what used to be our joint domicile on Robert Lane. In view of the fact that Twink is expecting Fang's baby within weeks of the scheduled nuptials, you might think a little more discretion was called for, but discretion has never been Fang's long suit. For that matter, it must not be Twink's, either, since the baby was conceived some time prior to my abandoning our marriage bed.

For those of you who are concerned about my state of mind as I approach this change in marital status, don't be. I'm fine. I'm ready to make a clean break of it; glad to have what was clearly my sham of a marriage—as far as Fang was concerned anyway—over and done with. I'm moving on with my new life. When you're doing that, hanging on to the old one doesn't help. Neither does bitterness. As my mother is prone to point out, bitterness destroys the container it's in.

If I do say so myself, this particular container is going to be in pretty fine shape tomorrow when I show up in court. With my son's help, I've been working out. My personal shopper at Nordstrom down in Scottsdale has set aside a couple of new outfits for me. I plan on picking up one of them on my way through the Phoenix area later on this afternoon.

In other words, for today anyway, I'm a rolling stone, and rolling stones gather no moss—and do no blogging.

Posted 7:23 A.M., September 15, 2005 by Babe

As soon as Ali Reynolds hauled her suitcase out of the closet, Samantha, Ali's now-permanent refugee cat, disappeared. Completely. Ali found it hard to believe that a sixteen-pound, one-eyed, one-eared cat could pull off that kind of magicianship, but she could.

Six months earlier, a series of forced moves had left Sam in a new, unfamiliar home with a new owner who wasn't exactly enamored of cats. Over time, Ali and Sam had developed a grudging respect for each other. With the unwelcome appearance of a suitcase, however, all bets were off. For Sam, the sight of a suitcase and/or the dreaded cat crate brought back all those bad old times and sent the panicky kitty scrambling for someplace to hide.

It took Ali a good two hours—two hours she didn't have—to find the animal again, scrunched in beside the drainpipe behind the washing machine in the laundry room. And finding Sam was only part of the problem. Extricating the cat from her snug little hidey-hole and into the cat crate for a trip to Ali's parents' place was a whole other issue. Had it been any other weekend, Sam could have remained at home and been looked after by Ali's son, Christopher, but it happened that Chris was due at a two-day seminar in Phoenix starting early Saturday morning.

"Off to Grandma's with you," Ali said, retrieving the indignant cat and stuffing her into the waiting crate. "And you'd better behave yourself, too."

And so, hours later than she had intended, Ali finally finished packing. With Sam yowling in bitter protest, Ali left her hilltop mobile home digs and drove her lapis blue Porsche Cayenne down to the highway, where she parked under the shady weeping willow tree outside her parents' family-owned diner, Sedona's fabled Sugar Loaf Café.

Inside, the lunch hour rush was just beginning. Edie Larson, Ali's mother, was working the cash register and lunch counter while Ali's father, Bob, held sway in the kitchen. Edie picked up an empty coffeepot and headed for the back counter to refill it, glancing reflexively at her watch as she did so.

"You call this an early start?" Edie asked.

Since Edie rose every morning at o-dark-thirty to prepare the Sugar Loaf's daily supply of signature sweet rolls, she considered any departure that happened after 6 A.M. to be tardy. She had thought Ali's initial estimated departure of nine to be close to slothful. Now it was coming up on noon.

"Unfortunately, Sam had other ideas," Ali said. "She saw the suitcase and went into hiding. I found her, though, finally."

"Good," Edie said reassuringly. "Cats usually don't like change, but by the time your father gets finished spoiling Sam, that ugly cat of yours won't even want to go back home. Where is she, by the way?"

"Out in the car in the shade."

Edie poured Ali a cup of coffee. "I'll call Kip to come get the crate and take Sam back to the house."

Kip Hogan was a formerly homeless Vietnam War vet Bob Larson had dragged home about the same time his daughter had adopted Sam. Originally Kip had been hired to help look after Bob in the aftermath of an unfortunate snowboarding accident that had left Ali's father temporarily wheelchair-bound. Bob had since recovered and was back at work, but Kip continued to hang around, living in an old Lazy Daze motor home parked in the Larsons' backyard, helping out with odd jobs around both the house and the restaurant, and gradually becoming more and more indispensable.

"Want some lunch before you go?" Edie asked. "Or should I have Dad make up one of the coolers for you to take along with you?"

"What would go in the cooler?" Ali asked.

"Fried chicken," Bob Larson answered from the kitchen service window. "Biscuits. Some homemade applesauce."

Having been raised on her father's crisp fried chicken and her mother's lighter-than-air biscuits, there was really no contest. "I'll have coffee now and take the cooler option," Ali answered.

Edie took a brief jaunt down the counter, delivering coffee as she went, then she returned to Ali. "Are you all right?" she asked.

"I'm perfectly fine," Ali said. "It'll be good to have this whole mess behind me."

"Yes," Edie agreed. "I'm sure it will be."

Ali had retreated to Sedona, her hometown, to find

her bearings in the initial aftermath of both losing her job and learning about her husband's infidelity. She hadn't expected to like it; hadn't expected to be comfortable there, but she was. The double-wide mobile home her aunt Evelyn had left her may have seemed like a big comedown from the gated mansion on Robert Lane, but it suited Ali's needs, everything from the Jacuzzi soaking tub to the basement wine cellar. And having her son, Chris, for a roommate didn't hurt, either.

Chris had graduated from UCLA and was in his first year of teaching welding and American history at Sedona High School. Ali enjoyed her son's company. He never left a mess in the kitchen, didn't stay out all that late, and spent much of his spare time working on his metal sculpting projects down in the basement. From what Ali could tell, she and Chris got along better than did many parents and their newly adult children.

All in all, she felt at ease being back home in Sedona—at ease and at peace.

"I wish Chris were going over with you," Edie added, seeming to read Ali's mind. "Driving to L.A. is a long trip to do all by yourself."

"Chris is busy with a seminar this weekend," Ali replied. "I don't mind driving. In fact, I enjoy being on the open road. Besides, I've got Aunt Evelyn's library of musicals along to keep me company."

"Well, be sure you take plenty of breaks," Edie cautioned. "They say tired drivers are as bad as drunk drivers."

Bob rang the bell, letting Edie know that an order was ready. While she went away to deliver it, Kip Hogan turned up at Ali's elbow. "Keys?" he asked.

When Kip had first appeared, six months earlier, he had come from a snowy, outdoor homeless encampment up on the Mogollan Rim. After years of living rough, he had been gaunt and grubby, with long, filthy hair, dirty clothes, missing teeth, and a much-broken nose. Kip's missing teeth and crooked nose were still at issue, but months of eating decent food had allowed him to fill out some. And dressed in respectable if secondhand clothing and with ready access to running water, the man looked far less scary than he had initially.

Without a word, Ali handed over her car keys.

"Leave the cat in her crate in the living room," Edie told Kip as he started for the door. "That way she'll have a chance to get used to her new digs before we let her out to explore."

"Yes, ma'am," Kip replied. "Will do."

"When will you be back?" Edie asked her daughter.

"Tuesday or Wednesday," Ali replied. "The divorce hearing is tomorrow. Then on Monday or Tuesday there's supposed to be a deposition in the wrongful dismissal suit. It didn't make sense to do two trips when one would work. So I'll stay over however long it takes to give the deposition."

"Good," Edie agreed. "It's always better to kill two birds with one stone. More coffee?"

Ali let her mother refill her cup. Initially she had blamed her tardy departure on Sam. Now Ali realized that she was stalling even more all on her own—and she knew why. Months after the fact, there was part of her that dreaded getting on I-17 and heading down to Phoenix. Ali Reynolds had almost died on one particularly dangerous stretch of that freeway when someone had tried to push her off the highway and over the edge of a sheer cliff. Being the target of an attempted murder is something that lingers, and even though Ali had driven that same route several times between then and now, she was still skittish. Just thinking about driving past the Sunset Point rest area and heading down the steep grade into the valley was enough to make Ali's hands go clammy.

Her face must have betrayed some of the concern she was feeling.

"Are you sure you wouldn't like some company?" Edie Larson asked solicitously. "And some moral support once you get there and have to go to court? I'm sure your father could manage without me for a day or two. He wouldn't like it, but having to get up early enough to make the rolls wouldn't kill him."

Touched by the offer, Ali smiled. "Thanks, Mom," she said. "I'll be fine. Really."

"And you'll call and let us know how it's going?"

"I promise."

Kip returned with her car keys, and Ali took her leave. She stopped by the bank and picked up some cash. She had a particular pet charity that she wanted to help along while she was in L.A., and she knew a cash gift would be most welcome.

A little less than an hour after leaving the bank, Ali was past the most worrisome stretch of the Black Canyon Freeway and headed into Scottsdale. At the time she had left her evening news gig in L.A., she had ditched her old newscasting wardrobe and her California persona like a snake shedding a cast-off skin. For as long as she'd been in Sedona, she'd worn her hair in a less-than-stylish ponytail and limited her wardrobe to what was comfortable—mostly sweatshirts and worn jeans. Now, though, facing courtroom appointments and the prospect of more than a little public notoriety, Ali understood that she needed to dress and look the part. Not only did she pick up several outfits, she stopped by one of Scottsdale's upscale salons for some much-needed pampering, including a haircut along with a spa-style mani/pedi.

Properly attired, coiffed, and accessorized, Ali felt ready to face what she had come to think of as her California ordeal. She headed west in late-afternoon, rush-hour traffic and soon found herself stuck in a jam of speeding eighteen-wheelers, all of them driving blindly but hell-bent-for-election into the setting sun. Tired of trying to stay out of their way, Ali pulled off at the first rest area she saw. There, sitting at a shaded picnic table, she opened her cooler. Not only was her father's carefully prepared food there, so was a collection of plastic utensils. With noisy traffic rushing by in the background, Ali savored her combination lunch/dinner of fried chicken and honey-slathered biscuits. Then, feeling fatigued and still not wanting to face into the glaring sunset, she returned to the Cayenne, locked the doors, lowered her seat back, and allowed herself the luxury of a nap.

She slept far longer than she expected. It was dark when she woke up, but she felt refreshed. Once back on the road, Ali was relieved to realize that traffic was noticeably lighter, and she was grateful she'd had the good sense to wait out the setting sun rather than driving into it.

Ali realized that that was one of the wonderful things about traveling on her own. She could eat when she was hungry, sleep when she was tired. It wasn't necessary to take anyone else's needs, wants, or opinions into consideration. Yes, being back on her own was definitely growing on Ali Reynolds.

She took her mother's advice to heart. When she stopped for gas in Blythe, she stopped at a roadside restaurant for coffee as well. She was halfway through the second cup when her phone rang.

"Well," Helga Myerhoff said in her distinctly gruff and smoky voice. "Have we girded our loins?"

Helga, sometimes called Rottweiler Myerhoff, had a not-undeserved reputation for being one of the Hollywood elite's premier divorce attorneys. With Helga's help and with the added impetus of Paul wanting a fast divorce as opposed to a cheap one, Ali had a generous divorce settlement coming to her, one that gave her pretty much everything she wanted. Between them Helga and Ali had, in fact, taken Fang to the cleaners.

Ali laughed. "They're girded, all right. New duds, new haircut, killer nails. Believe me, I'm ready."

"Good," Helga said. "And you're staying at the Westwood on Wilshire?"

"That's right," Ali answered. "I'm booked there through Tuesday. Marcella has a wrongful dismissal deposition coming up on either Monday or Tuesday. I'm staying over for that as well."

Marcella Johnson and Helga both worked for the same high-end legal firm, Weldon, Davis, and Reed, but the two women had wildly divergent styles and areas of expertise. Helga specialized in divorce cases. Marcella focused on employment issues. Ali counted herself fortunate to have not one but two dynamic attorneys on her team.

"Don't worry about tomorrow," Helga said. "We're in good shape on this and I'm pretty sure it'll go through without a hitch. Still, though, until everything's signed, sealed, and delivered, our agreement in principle could conceivably go south."

"Paul won't let that happen," Ali said with a laugh. "Not with his shotgun wedding set for Saturday. If something goes wrong with his walking April Gaddis down the aisle, there'll be hell to pay."

"You're all right then?" Helga asked.

Everyone seemed to be concerned about how Ali was holding up through all this. Why didn't anyone believe her when she said she was fine? She said it again, one more time and for the record.

"I'm fine, Helga. I wish people would stop worrying about me."

"Getting a divorce is stressful," Helga said.

"No," Ali corrected. "Compared to being married to a jerk, getting a divorce is easy."

"All right," Helga said. "See you in court, ten A.M. sharp. Judge Alice Tennant is very old-fashioned. She doesn't brook tardiness from anybody—attorneys or plaintiffs."

"Ten sharp," Ali repeated. "I'll be there."

Leaving Blythe, Ali turned up the volume on her MP3 player and sang along with the tunes from one musical comedy after another, from *A Connecticut Yankee* to *A Chorus Line*. As she drove, only a bare sliver of rising moon was visible in the rearview mirror behind her, but the nighttime sky was clear enough that even by starlight she could see the hulking forms of distant mountain ranges jutting up out of the silvery desert floor.

Crossing through California, Ali felt a strange disconnect. She had gone there years earlier with a new husband and a new job, following what had seemed then to be an American dream. Now, coming back to L.A. for the first time since that dream had exploded in her face, she realized that she was, literally, yesterday's news. Her job and her connection to her prominent network-exec husband had made her part of the L.A. in-crowd. This trip was the exact opposite. As an antidote, she turned up the music even louder.

Sometime around midnight, shortly after passing the exit to Twentynine Palms, Ali saw a whole phalanx of emergency vehicles surging eastbound and toward her on the freeway. Worried that debris from some unseen accident might litter the road ahead, Ali slowed, but then, one by one, the approaching vehicles veered off on what she knew to be the Highway 111 exit angling toward Palm Springs.

The emergency response was so massive that Ali found it worrisome. Wondering if maybe a plane had gone down, Ali turned off her original cast recording of *Camelot* and scanned through the radio dial until she found one of L.A.'s twenty-four-hour all-news channels. It was another ten minutes, after bits about Iraq and the latest riots in France, before the announcer cut in with a local news flash.

"The Riverside Sheriff's Department is investigating a possible train/vehicle collision on the eastbound tracks approaching Palm Springs. Emergency vehicles have been dispatched to the area and a CALTrans spokesman is suggesting that the area be avoided until further notice."

Relieved to hear that whatever was wrong didn't involve a problem on the freeway, Ali punched the "resume" button on her cruise control and took the Cayenne back up to speed. Then she switched off the news and went back to listening to King Arthur's bored and disaffected knights singing their rousing rendition of "Fie on Goodness."

As she drove past the Highway 111 interchange, the emergency vehicles had mostly stopped, forming a long, unbroken string of flashing red and yellow lights that erased the starlight and cast an eerie pulsing glow on the surrounding desert.

Ali drove on, thinking about trains and cars and what happens when one crashes into the other. In her days as a newbie television reporter, Ali had seen plenty of incidents like that, ones where people seemingly determined to opt out of the gene pool had decided, for one incredibly stupid reason or another, to try to outrun a speeding train, leaving behind a trail of bloody carnage and shattered metal. Sometimes the incidents included groups of teenagers playing a deadly game of chicken. Others drove onto the tracks deliberately and with the full intention of ending it all. Regardless of their motivation, the people in the vehicles usually didn't survive. Sometimes the engineers on the trains didn't make it out alive, either. The ones who did often lived out their days with a lifelong burden of guilt.

"At least this time it's got nothing to do with me," Ali

breathed aloud as she headed west toward Banning and Beaumont and the sprawling city of Los Angeles glowing far in the distance. "And thank God I don't have to report on it, either."

{ **CHAPTER 2** }

Helga called the next morning at eight. "So you know where you're going?" she asked.

Ali had lived in California for years. She knew her way around Beverly Hills. "The West District Courthouse, right?"

"Close, but no cigar," Helga said. "Your husband wanted this divorce in a hell of a hurry. In California, if you don't want to wait in line for court time, you can hire a private judge. I told him fine, as long as I got to choose the judge, which I did. Judge Alice Tennant's court is a few blocks away from there in what used to be a private residence."

"I didn't know there was any such thing as a private judge," Ali muttered.

"You do now," Helga returned.

Helga had referred to Alice Tennant's courtroom as a private residence, but the term hadn't done the place justice. *Mansion's more like it,* Ali thought an hour and a half later when she pulled up in front of the two-story porticoed edifice with lions guarding either side of a gated entrance complete with a circular drive. Helga was waiting on the front porch, pacing back and forth in front of a pair of Art Deco doors radiant with what looked like genuine Tiffany stained glass. Beyond the glass doors was a marbled foyer, its old-fashioned elegant ambience marred by the mundane and thoroughly modern presence of a wand-holding uniformed security guard and a metal detector.

They were directed into an ornate room that had probably once served as a formal dining room. A magnificent, hand-carved sideboard at the far end was covered with a silver coffee service, plates, cups, saucers, and silverware, and a collection of breakfast pastries that would have put most self-respecting hotel buffets to shame. The display came complete with a uniformed butler who handled the pouring.

Ali was sipping freshly squeezed orange juice and nibbling on a deliciously flaky croissant when Paul's attorney, Ted Grantham, came rushing into the room.

"Paul's still not here?" Grantham demanded of Helga.

"Not so far," Helga returned with a tight smile.

Ted Grantham was someone Ali knew slightly. He had been a guest at their Robert Lane home on several occasions, and he was a regular attendee at Paul's daylong Super Bowl extravaganzas. Now, though, Ted barely acknowledged her. Refusing offers of coffee, he paced back and forth in the entryway, making one brief cell phone call after another. By five to ten, when Paul had yet to arrive, Ted was downright frantic.

"So where's his bad boy?" Helga muttered under her breath. "Hope he's not planning on keeping the judge waiting."

But it turned out that was exactly what Paul seemed to have in mind. At three minutes after ten, a bailiff summoned all three of them into the judge's chambers.

Judge Alice Tennant was seated behind an immense partner desk that reminded Ali of one she'd seen in an antiques shop in the idyllic Cotswold town of Stow-on-the-Wold. Dwarfed by the desk, Judge Tennant was a sixty-something with flaming red hair and a temper to match.

"My time's very valuable, and you know I don't like being kept waiting, Mr. Grantham," she snapped as they filed into the room. "So where exactly is your client? Was he aware that he was expected here at ten this morning?"

"Yes, of course he knew," Grantham said hurriedly. "I've been trying to reach him all morning. He isn't answering any of his phones. The calls keep going straight to voice mail, and he hasn't called me back, either."

"I was given to understand there was some urgency about our doing this today," Judge Tennant observed. "About Mr. Grayson wanting to have his divorce finalized in a timely fashion."

Grantham looked uncomfortable. "Yes," he said. "There is something of a deadline."

"Because?"

Grantham glanced briefly in Ali's direction before he answered. "Well," he said reluctantly. "Actually, Mr. Grayson is due to be married tomorrow."

"I presume that would be to someone other than the wife who happens to be here right at the moment?"

Judge Tennant asked. Her sharp blue eyes focused fully on the squirming attorney, whose forehead, by then, had popped out in a very unlawyerly sweat.

"Yes," Grantham muttered. "That would be correct. To someone else. I'm sure I'll be able to locate my client in the next little while. If you could find a spot for us in this afternoon's calendar—"

Alice Tennant's reply was brisk. "There is no afternoon calendar. As it happens, I'm leaving town right after lunch," she said with a cold smile. "You'll have to check with my clerk to see if it's possible to reschedule for sometime next week—if that's all right with you, Ms. Reynolds. I understand you've driven all the way over from Arizona."

"Of course," Ali said quickly. "Next week will be fine. I want to stay on until this is sorted out."

"Excellent," Judge Tennant said.

"Perhaps you could see your way clear to hand this off to another judge—" Grantham began.

Helga started to object, but Judge Tennant silenced both attorneys with a single wave of her hand. "I was contracted to deal with this case," she said severely. "I have no intention of handing it off to anyone. Once the next court date is set, I trust you'll notify your client that he will be present on the appointed day and at the appointed hour. Please remind him that I may be a private judge, but I can nonetheless cite him for contempt of court. Is that clear, Mr. Grantham?"

"Yes, ma'am," Grantham replied contritely. "Quite clear."

"Just for the record," she added. "If I hear that any kind of marriage ceremony is performed tomorrow without your client being properly divorced from Ms. Reynolds beforehand, I'll see to it that he's charged with bigamy, which happens to be a criminal offense. Is that also clear?"

"Yes," Grantham said. "Very."

"All right then. See my clerk."

Ali couldn't help feeling a bit giddy at the idea that Paul's absence at the hearing had left Twink's lavish plans for her wedding day in utter shambles. Hurrying out into the corridor to wait while Helga Myerhoff and Ted Grantham dealt with the court clerk, she almost collided with a man rushing toward her from the security checkpoint.

"Ali!" he exclaimed. "Don't tell me the hearing's finished already."

Ali recognized the new arrival as Jake Maxwell, one of Paul's fellow network execs. She was surprised to see him there; surprised to think he'd squander some of his precious time on Paul's legal issues. Jake and his ditzy wife, Roseanne, weren't high on Ali's list of social acquaintances any more than Ted Grantham was.

"Hi, Jake," she said. "We're done for today. What brings you here?"

At least he had the good grace to look sheepish. "You know, moral support and all that."

"Well, you missed on that one," Ali said. "Paul didn't show."

Helga emerged from the courtroom wearing a grim smile. "Thursday morning. Ten A.M. again." Then, looking at Jake, she added derisively, "Oh, Mr. Maxwell, you must be Mr. Grayson's cheering section. I'm afraid the match has been rescheduled for next week—same time, same station. See you then." Dismissing Jake, Helga turned back to Ali. "Is that all right with you?"

"Thursday is fine," Ali said. "I can stay that long if I have to."

Ted Grantham entered the hallway. Jake quickly gravitated in his direction.

"Why isn't Paul here?" he asked.

"Beats the hell out of me," Grantham replied heatedly. "He blew off our court appearance, and now the judge is pissed at me."

"Did you check with April?"

"Of course I checked with April. She has no idea where Paul is. He never came home last night."

The glass doors closed behind the two men, taking the rest of the conversation outside with them.

"So he didn't come home last night," Helga observed. "Not good. Not good."

"It sounds amazingly familiar to me," Ali said.

"Well," Helga said, "if Paul Grayson knows what's good for him, he'll cancel his wedding and make the cancellation a media event all its own."

"Why? The bigamy thing? Would Judge Tennant really put him in jail for going through with the wedding?"

"Absolutely," Helga replied. "Alice Tennant takes a dim view of those kinds of marital shenanigans. Her ex, Jack, did the same thing, you see. Got married while the divorce decree was still warm to the touch—the same day, in fact. It's lucky for Paul—and for Ted Grantham, too—that we've already hammered out a property settlement."

Ali was astounded. "Why on earth did Paul agree to use her as a judge?"

"Because he was in a hurry," Helga answered. "Like I told you, I got to choose."

Just then, the glass entry doors swung open and a very tall black woman, clad in sweats and tennis shoes, entered the building. She paused briefly while going through the security checkpoint, then came trotting down the hall toward Ali and Helga.

"Am I too late?" the newcomer asked breathlessly, smothering Ali in a bone-crushing hug. "Sorry. I went to the courthouse and looked everywhere for the right courtroom before someone finally pointed me in this direction. Is it over already?"

"Not *over* over," Ali replied. "But it's over for today."

"Who's this?" Helga wanted to know.

"My cheering section," Ali replied with a smile. "My friend Sister Anne. And Sister Anne, this is my attorney, Helga Myerhoff."

At six foot seven, Sister Anne towered over both Ali and the diminutive Helga. She was dressed in blue-and-white UCLA insignia sweats and high-end Nikes and looked far more like the NCAA championship basketball player she had once been than the Sister of Charity she was now. Jamalla Kareem Williams had left college with a degree in business administration, plenty of basketball trophies, and a permanently damaged knee. Rather than going into business, she had become a nun. For years now, she had managed My Sister's Closet, a Pasadena-based clothing recycling program that helped provide appropriate, low-cost attire for impoverished women hoping to get into the job market. That was where Ali had dropped off her newscaster duds when she had left town months earlier.

Sister Anne held out her hand in Helga's direction. "Glad to meet you," she said with a gap-toothed smile while her beaded cornrows clicked and clattered around her head.

"Sister Anne and I met years ago at a charity fund-raiser and just hit it off," Ali explained. "In fact, if it weren't for her, I probably wouldn't know about you. Marcella Johnson was one of Sister Anne's basketball teammates at UCLA. When I was looking at filing a wrongful dismissal suit against the station, Sister Anne pointed me at Marcella, and when I needed a divorce attorney, Marcella sent me to you."

Sister Anne turned back to Ali. "What do you mean it's not *over* over?"

"My not-quite-ex didn't bother showing up for the hearing," Ali told her. "The new court date is set for Thursday of next week."

"Well, then," Sister Anne said briskly. "Let's go have some lunch."

Helga begged off, so Ali and Sister Anne drove to Beverly Center and had lunch in a Mexican restaurant where one of Sister Anne's recent clients from My Sister's Closet had hired on as the hostess. Over a shared plate of fajitas, Ali reached into her purse and pulled out an envelope, which she handed to Sister Anne.

"What's this?"

"Money," Ali said. "It's one thing to donate clothing, but this time I decided to give you something that would help pay the rent and keep the lights on."

Sister Anne counted through the bills, then looked up. "You can afford this?"

"Helga's a very good attorney. I'm going to be fine."

Smiling, Sister Anne slipped the envelope into a zippered pocket on her pants. "This couldn't come at a better time," she said. "We've been right on the edge of having to close the place down. You have no idea how much we needed this."

The hostess, a young Hispanic woman dressed in a stylish black dress and sling-back high heels—clothing that had been someone else's castoffs—smiled shyly at Sister Anne and Ali as she led a group of diners to a table.

"Glad I could help," Ali said. And she was.

After lunch, feeling a strange sense of letdown, Ali returned to her hotel. First she called her mother, who was still at the Sugar Loaf.

"Well?" Edie Larson said. "Are you free as a bird now?"

"Not exactly," Ali said, and then went on to explain the situation.

"My word," Edie said. "If that doesn't take the cake! After you had to drive all that way! It's inexcusable for him to not show up like that. Did you try calling him?"

"No," Ali admitted. "Under the circumstances, that didn't seem like a good idea. His attorney called, though. From what he was saying, it sounded like Paul stayed out all night."

"And he hasn't even married the poor girl yet?" Edie demanded. "Seems like it's a little early for him to be up to his old tricks."

Ali didn't exactly agree with the "poor girl" part. But

the "old tricks" reference worked. "Yes," Ali said. "It does seem early."

"You stay there as long as necessary in order to get this all straightened out," Edie said. "Everything here is under control. Chris stopped by last night before he headed for his seminar in Phoenix tomorrow. We invited him to come to dinner Sunday night when he gets home, so he won't starve to death. As for Sam? She's fine. She took to your father the way most strays do. In other words—love at first sight. What are you going to do with this extra time, hook up with some old friends?"

What old friends? Ali wondered. Other than Sister Anne, she didn't seem to have any real friends waiting for her. The ones she did have were people who were primarily friends of Paul's. In the aftermath of her blowup with Paul and the abrupt ending to her television career, Ali had been surprised and hurt by the number of people who had simply vanished from her life the moment her face had disappeared from the evening news. It had been hard to accept that people she had considered close friends had been drawn by her celebrity rather than anything else. Coming to terms with the reality of those lost relationships still hurt, but Edie Larson didn't need to know that.

"Already handled, Mom," Ali said as airily as she could manage. "Not to worry."

But it wasn't. When Ali got off the phone with her mother, she slipped out of her new Nordy's "court dress" and changed into a T-shirt and jeans. There were, of course, people she could have called, some of whom were bound to be in town. But she didn't call any of them. There was something so trite and Hollywoody—so whiny and pathetic—about gathering a group of pals around to hold your hand during stalled divorce proceedings that she couldn't bring herself to do it. Instead, Ali pulled out her computer and turned to Babe of Yavapai's new friends—the ones who were only a mouse click away.

CUTLOOSEBLOG.COM
Friday, September 16, 2005

Surprisingly enough it's more difficult to be cut loose legally than one would think. The divorce that was supposed to be finalized today isn't because my soon-to-be-former husband was a no-show in court, and our rent-a-judge refused to issue a decree without his being present and accounted for. So here I am stuck in limbo for a little longer. This should all be brought to a conclusion next week, but for now I'm here with time on my hands and not much to do.

In the past I've always had work to fall back on. And family responsibilities. But my son is raised now. I no longer have to look after him, and although I'm not entirely finished with him yet, I no longer have a husband to look after, either.

So I've decided to treat this like an extended vacation—a vacation in a place where I used to live, but where I was always too busy working to do the things tourists from around the world

come here to do. Starting with the Getty. And
the La Brea Tar Pits. Who knows? I may even
throw over the traces completely and go for a
walk on the beach or spend a day at Disneyland.

In other words, blogging will be light for
a while for the very good reason that I'm out
having fun.

Posted 2:16 P.M., September 16, 2005 by Babe

After that, Ali read through and posted some of the
comments that had come in from her readers while
she'd been otherwise engaged.

Dear Babe,
I know you're lawyer said your divorce would be
final, but don't you believe him. Divorces ain't
never final. They can give you a hundred pieces
of paper that say your single, but being married
don't just go away because of a piece of paper,
especially if you have kids. And I should know.
My husband can still drive me crazy even though
we've been divorced for fifteen years and hes been
dead for ten. If I end up still being married to
him when I get to heaven, I may just turn around
and walk right back out.

LILY

The next comment came from one of Ali's regu-
lars, a widowed longtime fan from California, who
wrote cheery little notes every other day or so. Over
the months, Ali had come to think of the woman as

a friend, despite the fact that they had never met in person.

> Dear Babe,
> I know this is a tough time for you. I just wanted you to know my thoughts and prayers are with you.
>
> VELMA T IN LAGUNA

Then there was Fred.

> What happened to "Whosoever God has joined together let no man put asunder"? No wonder the world is going to hell in a handbasket. First women wanted the Equal Rights Amendment and now they don't even want to bother with having husbands. And did you ever give any thought as to how you treated your husband and what might have driven him into the arms of another woman? I'm glad I only have sons and no daughters.
>
> FRED

So am I, Ali thought. She decided not to post Fred's comment. Then she changed her mind. She suspected there were a lot of people in the world who shared his opinion and regarded independent women as a direct threat to their manhood and to their very existence. Maybe that was something cutlooseblog needed to bring up as a topic of discussion.

Dear Babe,
My husband did the same thing, married his
little cutie two days after our divorce. It didn't
last. Two months later he was back, knocking
on my door because she'd thrown him out and
begging me to take him back, which I did. He
stayed for three more years after that then he left
again and now I don't know where he is. But I
know you're smarter than I am, so if your cheat-
ing husband asks you to take him back, whatever
you do, don't.

WISER NOW

Ali's phone rang. She recognized the number—the Flagstaff branch of the YWCA. "Hi, Andrea," Ali said.

Andrea was Andrea Rogers. A year ago, Andrea had been second in command in what was essentially a two-woman nonprofit spearheaded by Ali's girlhood best friend, Reenie Bernard. Reenie had been the outgoing, fund-raising brains of the outfit, while Andrea had functioned as office manager, keeping the place running smoothly in Reenie's absence. After Reenie's tragic murder, it had been Andrea who had tracked down Reenie's personal effects and, for the benefit of Reenie's orphaned children, rescued them from the thrift shop where they'd been shipped by Reenie's less-than-grief-stricken husband.

For Andrea, that one act of kindness on behalf of Reenie's kids had been the beginning of a new sense of self-confidence and independence. The Flagstaff YWCA had been so much Reenie Bernard's baby that, in the initial aftermath of her murder, there had been serious talk of shutting the place down, but Andrea in particular had been determined that Reenie's dream wouldn't perish with her. Over a period of several months, Andrea had managed to keep the doors open while Ali worked to convince the board of directors that, with a little assistance and encouragement from them, Andrea could be groomed to take over the executive director's position.

Her official promotion had happened three months ago. The board had hired a new assistant for Andrea, but Andrea had yet to catch on to the fact that she no longer needed to answer the phone herself—which she did most of the time.

Andrea was a plugger. She was dependable. She didn't have the finesse or the vision of a Reenie Bernard. What she had instead was an absolute devotion to her murdered boss and unbridled enthusiasm about carrying Reenie's life's work forward. One way or another, Andrea managed to get things done.

"Is it over then?" Andrea asked.

"'It' being the divorce?" Ali asked.

"Of course, the divorce," Andrea returned. "What else would I be asking about?"

"I'm beginning to wonder if my divorce will ever be over," Ali replied and went on to repeat the gory details one more time.

"But what if you're not home in time for the board meeting next Friday?" Andrea asked, as a hint of her old reticence crept into her voice. "I've never handled one of those by myself. I've always had you there to backstop me."

"I'll do what I can to be home by then," Ali said. "But if I'm not, you'll be fine. You know more about what's going on at the YWCA than anyone. You'll be able to handle it."

"I hope so," Andrea said, but she didn't sound convinced.

Ali was talking on her cell phone. It surprised her when the room phone began to ring. "Sorry, Andrea," Ali said. "I need to take that."

"Ms. Reynolds?" a woman's voice asked.

"Yes."

"My name is Detective Carolyn Little," she said. "I'm with the LAPD's Missing Persons Unit. Mr. Ted Grantham said you were staying at the Westwood, and I took the liberty of calling."

"About?" Ali asked.

"About your husband."

"My soon-to-be-former husband," Ali corrected.

"Are you aware he's missing?"

"I know he failed to show up in court this morning for our divorce hearing," Ali answered. "That's all I know."

"He's been reported missing by one April Gaddis."

"His fiancée," Ali supplied.

"Yes," Detective Little answered. "She did mention that she and Mr. Grayson are engaged. It seems he went to a bachelor party last evening and never came home."

Ali felt like mentioning that for Paul to declare himself a bachelor prior to his divorce being finalized was a bit like putting the cart before the horse, but Detective Little didn't sound like she had much of a sense of humor.

"When was the last time you saw your husband?" Detective Little asked.

"That would be Friday, March eleventh of this year," Ali answered at once.

There was a slight pause. "March eleventh? That's a long time ago—six months, but you still remember the exact date?"

"And the exact time," Ali responded. "I had just lost my job. I came home, expecting some sympathy from my husband, but in our house, you find sympathy in the dictionary between 'shit' and 'syphilis.' He took off with his girlfriend bright and early the next morning before I even woke up."

The "shit and syphilis" reference was one of her father's more colorful expressions, one that was guaranteed to send Bob Larson's wife into a spasm. Even Carolyn Little chuckled a little at that, so the woman wasn't entirely devoid of humor.

"This same girlfriend?" the detective added. "The fiancée?"

"Yes," Ali agreed. "That would be the one—the same one who's expecting his baby."

"And you came to town when?"

"Last night," Ali said. "I drove over from Sedona yesterday afternoon. I got a late start. It was almost two in the morning before I finished checking in."

"And you're here until?"

"Paul and I have another court date scheduled for next week."

"On Thursday," Little said. Obviously she had already acquired the information from Ted Grantham.

"And you'll be staying at the Westwood? And is there another number in case I need to reach you again?"

It had been six months since Ali had seen Paul Grayson, and she didn't see why the Missing Persons Unit would need to speak to her again, but she gave the detective her cell phone number all the same.

As Ali ended the call with Detective Little, she was already groping for the television remote. Within minutes of turning on the set she located a news tease from Annette Carrera, Ali Reynolds's blond, blue-eyed, surgically enhanced news anchor successor. The promo was already in progress when Ali tuned in: " . . . network executive who disappeared from his bachelor party last night. We'll have the story for you live on the evening news."

Carrera! Ali had to give credit to whoever had dreamed up that name. It was calculated to be high-toned enough to appeal to L.A.'s Porsche-craving yuppies, but it also sounded vaguely Hispanic—if you didn't look too closely at the blond hair, blue eyes, and fair skin. In Ali's not-unbiased opinion, Annette was far too young and far too perky. Her hair looked as if she had stuck her finger in an electrical outlet and then moussed the resulting hairdo into a froth of permanent peaks—like whipped cream beaten to a turn.

Disgusted at the idea of having to wait another two hours to glean any additional details, Ali reached for her computer, intent on surfing the Net to track down a breaking-news Web site. As she touched the keyboard, though, she heard a new-mail alert. She paused long enough to read the new message.

Dear Babe,
I just saw a news blurb on your old channel. I've
gone back to watching them even though I hate
that new Annette person. Anyway, it said a
man named Paul Grayson, some network big-
wig, is missing. I seem to remember that was
your husband's name. So is this your Paul
Grayson or is it just someone with the same
name?

VELMA T IN LAGUNA

No matter who he is, he isn't my Paul Grayson, Ali
thought, but she sent Velma an immediate response.

Dear Velma,
Thanks for bringing this to my attention. The
missing man most likely is "my" Paul Grayson.
Once I have more details on the situation, I'll try
to let you know.

BABE

{ **CHAPTER 3** }

For the next while, Ali surfed the Net. Her years in
L.A. had taught her that Southern California news
outlets had an insatiable appetite for anything involving

the entertainment industry—movies or television. Paul Grayson was high enough up the network food chain that it wasn't long before Ali found what she was looking for, even though it offered little more information than she had gleaned from the earlier news promo.

NBC EXEC MISSING

Paul Grayson, long considered NBC's West Coast go-to guy, has gone missing after an early and abrupt departure from his own bachelor party at the stylish Pink Swan on Santa Monica Boulevard in West Hollywood. His red Porsche Carrera was found stripped and abandoned in an apartment parking lot in Banning early this afternoon.

There it was again. Everybody seemed free to refer to Paul as a bachelor, despite the inconvenient fact that he was still legally married—to Ali. And what exactly was this "stylish" Pink Swan? Probably some cheesy strip joint or pole-dancing outfit. Whatever it was, the name sounded suitably sleazy. The next paragraph, however, shook her.

A spokesman for LAPD's Missing Persons Unit said they have reason to believe that Mr. Grayson has been the victim of foul play.

"Foul play." Ali repeated the words aloud. The very possibility that Paul had been victimized made Ali's earlier conversation with Detective Little seem much more ominous.

Jake Maxwell, who co-hosted the bachelor party, said the guest of honor departed early on in the proceedings. "Somewhere around ten or so, Paul went outside to take a phone call and didn't come back. Everyone was having a good time. It was a while before anyone noticed that he hadn't returned."

Because everyone was too blasted to notice, Ali thought. The news item ended. For several long minutes afterward, Ali wondered what, if anything, she should do. Finally, however, it seemed reasonable to let her divorce attorney know that Paul had now been declared a missing person. Ali picked up her cell phone and dialed Helga Myerhoff's number.

"What's up?" Helga asked.

"I thought you should know Paul didn't just miss his court appearance this morning," Ali told her attorney. "He disappeared from what they're calling his 'bachelor party' last night. There's some suspicion that foul play may be involved. His Carrera was found abandoned in an apartment house parking lot in Banning this afternoon."

Helga was all business. "How did you find this out?"

"Part of it I learned just now from reading a breaking-news Web site. The rest of it, though, came from a phone call from Detective Carolyn Little of the LAPD Missing Persons Unit."

"Why did she call you?" Helga asked. "And, beyond that, how did she even know to call you?"

"Since I hadn't seen Paul in more than six months, I thought it was odd that she'd be asking me for information, but Ted Grantham evidently told the detective I was in town and where I was staying."

Ali heard a slight rustling on the phone and could picture Helga standing behind her desk and squaring her shoulders, bristling to her diminutive but tough-as-nails five foot two. "What exactly did this detective say? And what's her name again?"

"Detective Carolyn Little, LAPD Missing Persons. She asked when I had arrived, why I was here, where I was staying, when did I last see Paul. All the usual stuff, I guess."

"Did she mention the possibility that you might be under any kind of suspicion?"

The severity of Helga's tone put Ali on edge and made her wonder if perhaps Detective Little's questions weren't quite so "usual" after all.

"Me?" Ali demanded, dumbfounded. "Why on earth would I be a suspect?"

"Has Paul changed his will?" Helga asked.

"I have no idea about that," Ali said. "We're getting a divorce, remember? I've rewritten my will so Chris is my primary beneficiary in case anything happens to me. I would assume Paul has done the same thing in favor of April and her baby."

"Not necessarily," Helga mused. "In my experience, men often put off handling those pesky little details."

"What are you saying?" Ali asked.

"Let's assume the worst," Helga said. "Let's say Paul Grayson turns up dead, a victim of some kind of foul play. If you and he aren't divorced—and you're not—and if, by some chance, his will hasn't been rewritten, it's likely you'll make out far better as a widow than you would have as a divorcée. From an investigative point of view and considering the dollar amounts involved, that might well put you at the top of the suspect list in a murder-for-profit scheme."

"Me?" Ali asked. "How is that possible? I had nothing to do with any of this—nothing at all. Besides, at the time Paul disappeared from his so-called bachelor party, I was out in the middle of the desert, somewhere this side of Blythe."

"Let's don't push panic buttons then," Helga reassured her. "We'll just sit back and see what happens. But, in the meantime, don't talk to any more detectives without having your attorney present."

"My attorney," Ali repeated. "You mean you?"

"No. Not me. I do divorces. I don't do criminal law," Helga continued. "That's a whole other can of worms. Not to worry, though. Weldon, Davis, and Reed has several top-drawer criminal attorneys on staff. I'll get a recommendation and have one of them be in touch with you."

Great, Ali thought. *Just what I need. Another frigging attorney!*

Once she was off the phone, Ali paced for a while. Finally, she lay down on the floor and forced herself to do some relaxation exercises. After settling some of her agitation, she climbed up on the bed. She never expected to fall asleep, but she did, waking just in time to switch on the local news. Out of force of habit, she turned once again to her old station.

Of course, the amazingly perky and spike-haired Annette Carrera was front and center, but so was the rest of the old news gang. The foppish Randall James, still wearing his appallingly awful wig, continued on as co-anchor. There, too, was Axel Rodbury, who, false teeth and all, had to be older than God. If Ali was considered over the hill, why wasn't he? And there was Bill Nickels, too, the leering and always overly enthusiastic sportscaster. Ali had wanted to smack the smug grin off his face for years, especially after hearing rumors that, when it came to student interns, Mr. Sports Guy had a tendency to try for a home run.

Ali had steeled herself for the ordeal, expecting that seeing her old colleagues gathered in the familiar confines of the newsroom set would hit her with some sense of loss. But as the quartet yucked it up in the required and supposedly unscripted pre-newscast lead-in, Ali wasn't at all surprised to see that Bill Nickels and Annette seemed to have an especially chummy relationship.

Don't you have brains enough to aim a little higher than that? Ali thought. *Not that aiming higher did me any good.*

Beyond that, though, she felt nothing at all. Nothing. Her leaving may not have been of Ali Reynolds's own volition, but as it turned out, she really had moved on. Whatever had happened, she was over it—except for her wrongful dismissal lawsuit. She wasn't over that—not by a long shot.

The lead story, introduced by Annette herself, had to do with Paul Grayson's disappearance. This was, after all, the NBC affiliate, and Grayson was a high-profile NBC bigwig. A young female reporter—one Ali had never seen before—delivered a brief story filmed in front of the gated entrance to the house on Robert

Lane. That, Ali knew, would send Paul utterly ballistic once he got wind of it. Having your front gate identified on television news for all the world to see was not good from a security standpoint.

The second, related segment, done by a roving reporter, was filmed in the paved parking lot of a less-than-desirable apartment complex somewhere in Banning. Of course, by the time the filming occurred, Paul's Arena Red 911 had already been towed away. Yellow crime scene tape was still visible but the vehicle wasn't, as the reporter earnestly let viewers know that this was where Paul Grayson's abandoned Porsche had been found early in the afternoon.

By the time the two segments were over almost three minutes of news time had elapsed and Ali had learned almost nothing she hadn't known before from simply surfing the Net.

"Useless," Ali muttered under her breath. She was close to changing the channel when part of a story Randall James was relating penetrated her consciousness. This one concerned an unidentified man found dead in the desert late Thursday night in the aftermath of a fatal train/vehicle collision that had occurred northwest of Palm Springs. Since Ali had been in such proximity to the incident when it happened, she stayed tuned to see the remainder of the piece.

The smiling faces on the tube, reading blandly from their teleprompters, didn't seem to make any connection between that case and the one they had reported on two stories before, and why should they? After all, they were paid to read what was given to them—stories that had already been written and edited by someone else. Connecting dots was never a required part of the news desk equation.

But Ali's life had undergone a fundamental change months earlier when she had started trying to piece together the details that would explain the sudden death of her friend Reenie Bernard. And now, this newly reconstituted Ali Reynolds was incapable of *not* connecting dots, especially when they were this obvious.

The body of an unidentified man found outside Palm Springs? Paul's abandoned vehicle located in a parking lot somewhere in Banning, ten or fifteen miles away? Without knowing how, Ali understood immediately that the two incidents were connected. She knew in her bones that the dead man found near Palm Springs had to be Paul. The only remaining question was, how long would it take for someone else to figure it out?

The answer to that question wasn't long in coming. Before Axel could launch into his weather report, there was a sharp rap on Ali's door.

"Who is it?" she asked, peering out through the security peephole. Two men wearing white shirts, ties, and sports jackets stood in the hall. One was white and older—mid-fifties—with a bad comb-over and the thick neck of an aging football player. The other was younger—mid-thirties, black, with a shaved head and the straight-shouldered bearing of an ex-Marine.

"Police," the older one said, holding up a wallet that contained a badge and photo ID. "Detectives Sims and Taylor, Riverside Sheriff's Department. We need to speak to you about your husband."

Helga Myerhoff's warning should have been uppermost in Ali's head, but it wasn't. Shaken by her sudden realization that Paul really was dead, she unfastened the security chain and opened the door.

"Is he dead?" she asked.

"He may be," Detective Sims, the older one, said. "That's why we need to speak with you. May we come in?"

Ali opened the door and allowed the two men into her room. Their looming presence combined with the weight of the news they carried filled what had previously seemed to be a spacious area. Ali retreated to a nearby chair. The detectives remained standing.

Ali's mind raced. She remembered the desolate desert, the darkness, the flashing emergency lights. She had driven Highway 111 into Palm Springs numerous times. She remembered the tracks running alongside the roadway. On the other side of the tracks was nothing—only desert. There was no reason to cross the tracks there, unless . . .

"This is about that car that got run over by the train last night, isn't it?" she said. "What happened? Did Paul commit suicide?"

The two detectives exchanged glances. "You're aware of the incident then?" Detective Sims asked.

"The incident with the train?" Ali asked. "Sure. It was on the news just now. So was the story about Paul. When I saw that his Porsche had been found stripped and abandoned in a parking lot in Banning, I put two and two together."

"That's what we're doing, too," Detective Taylor said, "putting two and two together. We have an unidentified victim we *believe* to be your husband, but we're not sure. Detective Little from LAPD told us where to find you. We need someone to do a positive ID."

"I'll get my purse," Ali said, standing up. "Where do you want me to go?"

"To the morgue," Sims said quickly. "In Indio."

"But that's hours from here, on the far side of Palm Springs."

"Riverside is a big county," Taylor returned. "That's where they've taken the body. But don't worry about how far it is. We'll be glad to take you over and bring you back. It's the least we can do."

Ali's purse was on the desk. Her Glock 26 was locked away in her room safe. She had left it there that morning when she was on her way to court, and she was glad it was still there. Even though she had a properly issued license to carry, it was probably not a good idea to show up in a cop car with a loaded handgun in her possession. Ali collected her purse and her cell phone.

"Let's go then," she said.

People glanced warily at the trio as they walked through the Westwood's well-appointed lobby. Ali was in the middle with the two cops flanking her on either side. Detectives Sims and Taylor may not have been in uniform, but they were still clearly cops. Outside, the real giveaway was the plain white, well-used Crown Victoria parked directly in front of the hotel entrance. Sporting a rack of two-way-radio antennas and black-wall tires, the Crown Victoria stuck out like a sore thumb next to its nearest neighbors—a silver Maserati Quattroporte and a gleaming black Bentley GT.

Sims opened the back door of the sedan to let Ali inside. When she saw there was no door handle, she felt a moment of concern. She realized belatedly that she probably should have called Helga before agreeing to come along with Sims and Taylor. Presumably Helga would have warned her against getting into a vehicle with them.

On the other hand, why not? Ali thought. *All they need is for me to identify the body. What's wrong with that?*

Ali remembered times in the past when she'd been assigned to cover ongoing police investigations. She remembered instances where some of the people involved refused to cooperate or to give statements of any kind to investigating officers without having an attorney present. And even though at the time Ali had known full well that was everyone's legal right, she had still harbored a sneaking suspicion that people who hid behind their attorneys had something else to hide as well.

Well, I don't, Ali told herself firmly. Settling into the backseat, she fastened her seat belt. While Detective Taylor drove, Sims rode shotgun and chatted her up.

"I understand from Detective Little that you and your husband are in the process of getting a divorce?"

Are getting *a divorce?* Ali wondered. The use of the present tense was telling. Until the detectives had a positive identification of their victim, they were going to hold firm to the fiction that Paul Grayson was still alive.

"Yes," Ali answered. "It was supposed to be finalized today. That was probably the first time anyone besides April noticed Paul was missing—when he didn't show up for the hearing."

"Friendly?" Sims asked.

At first Ali wasn't sure what Sims meant. "I beg your pardon?"

"You know," he responded. "Your divorce. Is it amicable and all that?"

"As amicable as can be expected considering my husband's girlfriend—his fiancée—is eight and a half months pregnant."

"With his baby?" Sims asked.

"So I've been told," Ali said. "They were supposed to get married tomorrow. Speaking of which, why am I doing the identification? Why not April?"

"You're still married to him," Sims said. "From our point of view, you're a surviving relative. She's not."

Ali thought about that for a few moments. It was rush hour. Traffic was painfully slow. As they inched along, Ali realized that she and the two detectives were in the same situation. They wanted information from her; she wanted the same from them.

"This man who's dead," she said, "this man who may be Paul. What was he doing on the railroad tracks? Did he go there on purpose? Was he trying to commit suicide or something? Maybe he and April had a fight and it pushed Paul over the edge."

"It wasn't suicide," Sims replied.

"An accident then?"

Sims said nothing.

Ali thought about what Jake had reportedly said about Paul bailing on his own bachelor party without bothering to tell his host or anyone else that he was leaving. Unless . . . Paul Grayson had never had a good track record where women were concerned. Ali could well imagine him picking up one of the strippers or the pole dancers or whatever brand of feminine charm the Pink Swan had available and taking her somewhere for a little private tête-à-tête.

"Was he alone or was he with someone?" Ali asked.

"We're not sure," Sims said. "We have people doing a grid search, but so far no other victims have been found."

There was a short pause before Detective Taylor piped up. "When exactly did you get to town, Ms. Reynolds? And did you drive over or fly?"

Taylor's questions activated a blinking caution light in Ali's head. She considered her words carefully before she answered. The very fact that she'd been close enough to see the flashing lights on the emergency vehicles might give the cops reason to think she was somehow involved. If she told them about driving past Palm Springs at midnight and seeing the lights, Sims and Taylor could well turn Ali's coincidental proximity into criminal opportunity. Still, she'd already given the same information to Detective Little. It seemed foolhardy to withhold it a second time, and there was even less point to not being truthful.

"I drove over yesterday," Ali said. "Last night. I left Phoenix late in the afternoon. Got to the hotel around two in the morning."

"Which means you were driving through the Palm Springs area around . . . ?"

"Midnight," Ali answered without waiting for Detective Taylor to finish posing his question. "And you're right. I did see the cop cars and ambulances and other emergency vehicles showing up at the scene of the wreck. It's dark in the desert. You could see those lights for miles. Later on, I heard on the radio that a train had crashed into a car."

Ali's cell phone rang just then. The phone number wasn't one she recognized. "Hello?"

"Ali Reynolds?"

"Yes."

"My name is Victor, Victor Angeleri. My colleague Helga Myerhoff asked me to call you. Sorry I couldn't get back to you earlier. I've been tied up in a meeting. I thought maybe it would be a good idea for us to get together so I could have a little better feel for what's happening. Helga gave me a brief overview, but I'd like a few more details from you. Since the office is just down the street from your hotel, I thought maybe I could drop by in a little while before I head home."

"Sorry," Ali said. "That won't be possible." She was aware that the cops in the front seat were listening avidly to everything she said and to every nuance of her side of the conversation. Their interest gave Ali a hint about how badly she had screwed up by not heeding Helga's advice.

"Why not?" Angeleri wanted to know. "What's more important than meeting with me?"

"It's just that I'm not at the hotel right now," she said. "I'm actually on my way to Indio. Two detectives from the Riverside Sheriff's Department picked me up and asked me to come with them. They need someone to identify a dead man—the man they think is my husband."

Angeleri uttered a string of very unlawyerlike words, ones Edie Larson would have deemed unprintable. "Are you nuts or what? You mean you just got in the car with them?" he demanded. "And now they're taking you all the way to Indio?"

Ali didn't know Victor Angeleri, but he sounded upset—furious, even—as though he couldn't quite believe he'd been stuck with such a numbskull for a client. Ali couldn't believe it, either.

"That's where the body is," Ali said.

"You're going to the coroner's office there?" Victor wanted to know.

"Evidently," Ali answered meekly.

"All right," Victor shouted into her ear. "Where are you now?"

"Merging onto the Ten."

"I'm leaving the office right now. I'll meet you there. In the meantime, keep your mouth shut."

"Where did you say we're going?" Ali asked, directing her question at Sims.

"The Riverside County Morgue," he answered. "The address is—"

"I know the address," Angeleri interrupted, bellowing the words loud enough to break Ali's eardrum. "I'll be there as soon as I can. Until you and I have a chance to talk in private, you're to say nothing more. Nothing! You can talk about the weather. You can talk about the World Series, but that's it. Understand?"

"Got it," Ali answered. "I hear you loud and clear."

That was actually something of an understatement since Sims and Taylor must have heard him, too. The two detectives exchanged a raised-eyebrow look, and Sims heaved a resigned sigh. Clearly they had been having their way with her. Now the game was up. Ali's only hope was that Victor Angeleri would be smart enough to dig her out of the hole she had dug herself into before she made it any deeper.

Ali glanced at her watch. At the rate traffic was moving, it would be another two hours before they made it to Indio. And with Victor leaving the office on Wilshire that much behind them, Ali calculated that it would be hours before the attorney could catch up with them. That meant she was in for several uncomfortable hours of keeping her mouth shut.

Gradually traffic began to thin. The car sped up, but clearly Taylor and Sims had gotten the message. They made no further attempt to ask her questions about anything—including the run-up to the World Series. Left to her own devices, Ali spent the time trying to figure out how, in the course of one short day, she had gone from being an almost divorced woman to being a homicide suspect.

Ali checked her watch when they pulled up outside the coroner's office in Indio. She expected they'd have to wait another hour at least before Victor could possibly catch up with them. Then, after however long it took to do the identification and conduct any additional interviews, there would be another three-hour car ride back to the hotel.

Resigned to the idea that it was going to be a very long night, Ali was astonished when an immense man rose from a small waiting room sofa and hurried toward them.

"Ali Reynolds?" he asked.

Assuming this was yet another cop of some kind, Ali nodded.

"Good," the newcomer said, turning to the detectives. "If you don't mind, I'd like a word in private with my client."

"We'll be right outside," Detective Sims replied before he and Taylor returned the way they had come.

"You're Victor?" Ali asked. "My attorney?"

He nodded. Victor may have served as the attorney to some of Hollywood's "beautiful people," but beautiful he was not. Victor was a wide-load kind of guy—John Candy wide—with droopy jowls and a receding hairline. His suit may have been expensive, but it didn't quite meet around his considerable girth. In one hand he carried a scarred, much-used leather satchel–style briefcase that was crammed to overflowing with papers.

"We left long before you did," Ali said. "How did you manage to get here first?"

"I chartered a plane from Santa Monica," he answered. He led her back to the sofa and placed his briefcase on the floor beside it. "Flew from Santa Monica Municipal to Jacqueline Cochran Regional here in Palm Springs. Believe me, at my hourly rate, it would be a total waste of your money for me to spend six billable hours driving back and forth to Indio. Now sit down here," Victor continued, indicating a place next to him on the sofa. "I need to know what's going on."

Too tired to object, Ali sat. She had been through enough emotional upheaval in the course of the day that she was feeling frayed and close to tears. When Victor reached for his briefcase, she expected him to extract either a hanky for her or else a laptop computer for him. Instead, he removed a dog-eared tablet of blue-lined paper. Reaching into his shirt pocket, he retrieved a black and white Montblanc fountain pen.

Over the past few years, Ali had come to rely on computers more and more. Somehow, though, she found it strangely reassuring to see that Victor Angeleri was not a high-tech kind of guy—that when it came time to do a job, he relied on brainpower and old-fashioned pen and paper. That was exactly what Ali Reynolds needed right then—not someone blessed with good looks or glitz or style, but someone with substance—someone who would be big enough and tough enough to take on the combined girth of Detectives Sims and Taylor and win.

"All right then," Victor said, removing the cap from his pen. "Tell me everything—from the beginning."

{ CHAPTER 4 }

CUTLOOSEBLOG.COM
Saturday, September 17, 2005

It's after one. I should be sleeping, but I can't. I didn't expect yesterday to be a good day. You know before it starts that the day you go to court to get a divorce isn't going to be a red-letter day or a time for celebration. But I didn't expect it to be a disaster, either. I didn't expect it to end with a trip to the morgue.

Because, although my divorce wasn't finalized yesterday, my marriage ended anyway. My husband is dead. He didn't show up for our ten A.M. court appearance because he died the night before—died after taking an early powder from his own bachelor party and departing the premises without telling anyone else he was leaving.

After spending hours in the company of a pair of homicide detectives, I now know how Fang died. His hands and feet were bound with duct tape. His mouth was taped shut. He was placed in the trunk of a stolen car that was left parked on the railroad tracks near Palm Springs. The vehicle with him in it was subsequently struck and demolished by a speeding freight train. He was ejected upon impact and thrown into the desert, where his body was found hours later. The autopsy won't be done until much later today. My hope is that he died upon impact.

And so, since the divorce was never finalized, the authorities consider me to be his "next of kin." For the first time in my life, I had to go to a county morgue to make a positive ID.

I expected the place to be dingy and cold inside. It wasn't, but the chill I felt had nothing to do with an overly active air-conditioning unit because the air-conditioning unit was barely

functioning. As I stood there in the viewing
room, waiting for an attendant to wheel out the
loaded gurney, my blood turned to ice. And when
I had to look down into that scratched and bat-
tered but oh-so-familiar face, it was all I could
do to remain upright. I didn't exactly faint when
I saw him lying there, but my knees went weak.
Fortunately, someone helped me to a chair.

I didn't cry, couldn't cry. Mostly because I
didn't know what I was feeling or what I was
supposed to feel. Fang and I were divorcing if
not divorced. Our relationship was over if not
ended. And yet, this was a man I had loved
once—someone vital and strong with whom
I had hoped to share the rest of my life. It
makes my heart ache to know that he is gone.
And yes, it makes me sick to think that his
unborn child—a baby due within the next
few weeks—will never know him at all, will
grow up without ever once seeing him. That's
wrong. Leaving a child fatherless is WRONG!
WRONG! WRONG!

After I'd done the ID, someone—a clerk—
gave me a paper to sign—a form that says what's
supposed to happen to Fang's remains once the
authorities are finished with them. It seemed
inappropriate for me to be the one deciding
which mortuary should be brought in to do
that job. I've been out of Fang's life for a long
time—longer, it turns out, than the six months
I've been out of the house. It seemed to me that
Twink . . . No, correction. Make that, it seemed

to me that his fiancée—the woman who's expecting his child—should be making those decisions, but it turns out the very fact that we were still legally married automatically puts me in charge. So I looked in the phone book, tracked down the name of the mortuary that handled Fang's mother's services six years ago, and called them.

Two days ago—was it just two days?—I told you about my plan to pick up some new clothing on my way through Scottsdale so I could go to court looking like a bit of a fashion plate in something more sophisticated than what I wear hanging around home in Sedona. I even splurged on a haircut, a manicure, and a pedicure. I wanted to be able to put my best foot (and toes) forward when Fang and I stood in front of the judge to disavow our vows.

The irony is, when I came back to the hotel, I took off my courtroom duds and slipped into something comfortable—a T-shirt, a pair of jeans, comfy tennis shoes. I took off my makeup and pulled my hair back into a ponytail. That's how I was dressed when two homicide cops came to ask me to ride along and see if I could positively identify the body of their dead victim. And that's how I looked hours later when the identification ordeal was finally over and I stepped back outside the Riverside County Sheriff's Substation in Indio to return to the hotel.

I have no idea who alerted the media to what was going on. I know for sure someone had already leaked Fang's name. As cameras flashed and reporters yelled questions, someone recognized me and called me by name as well. I'm sure my photo will be all over the news tomorrow, and I'll look as bedraggled as some of those awful mug shots that turn up when some celebrity gets booked for drunk driving.

It's one thing to stand outside the emotional box and report on someone's untimely death for whatever reason. It's something else to be living it—to be inside that awful box and trying to make sense of it. Now, because of the way the media works, I'll no longer be reporting on events—I'll be part of the story.

So this is an early warning for all my cutlooseblog.com fans. I'm sure all kinds of crap is going to hit the fan first thing in the morning. I just want you to know that I'm fine. And I'll keep you posted as we go.

Posted 1:07 A.M., September 17, 2005 by Babe

Scrolling through her e-mail list, Ali could see more than a dozen comments lined up and waiting to be read, but she was too drained to face them.

Go to bed, she told herself, switching off her computer. *Tomorrow's another day.*

Ali did go to bed then. Not only that, she surprised herself by falling asleep almost immediately. After what seemed like only a matter of minutes, the ringing phone awakened her.

"What in the world is going on?" Edie Larson demanded.

"What are you talking about?" Ali grumbled grog-
gily. "And what time is it?" The room's blackout curtains
were pulled shut. In the pitch-black room she had to
turn over to see the clock, which read 5:35 A.M.

"Why didn't you call me?" Edie continued. "What
happened to Paul? And why did you have to do the
identification? What about his bride-to-be who isn't?"

"Who told you all this?" Ali asked.

"You did," Edie answered. "In cutloose."

Ali was astonished. It had never occurred to her that
her mother might join the Internet world. "You read my
blog?" she asked.

"Of course I do," Edie said. "Why wouldn't I? Every
morning while I'm waiting for the sweet rolls to rise and
when there's no one here in the restaurant to keep me
company, I read the whole thing. When Dad and I got
Chris that new Mac, he gave us his old one. Hooked
it up here in the office, got me an Internet account,
the whole nine yards. My Internet handle is sugarloafmama, by the way, but I didn't call to talk about me. I
want to know what's going on with you. Tell me everything, and hurry it up. We open in a few minutes."

So Ali told her mother as much as she could remember—the parts she had put in the blog as well as the
parts she'd left out. The truth is, after sitting through
the statement she'd given to Detectives Sims and Taylor, Victor had advised her to say nothing in her blog
about any of it—nothing at all. Feeling a certain loyalty
to her readers, Ali had written her blog entry anyway,
saying only what she thought would pass muster. She
never came right out and said that she had ridden to
Indio in the company of the two homicide detectives.

And she never breathed a word about hitching a ride back from Jacqueline Cochran Airport with the newest member of Ali's burgeoning troop of attorneys.

In talking to Edie, however, Ali corrected this deliberate oversight by mentioning Victor Angeleri by name, while at the same time somehow glossing over the criminal defense portion of his curriculum vitae.

"You say his name's Victor, Victor Angeleri? What kind of a name is that?" Edie wanted to know.

"Italian, I suppose," Ali answered.

"And he flies his own plane?"

"No. He chartered one." *And on the way home, to take my mind off my troubles, gave me an in-depth lesson on Jacqueline Cochran, the lady the airport is named after, and on the Women Airforce Service Pilots of World War II,* Ali thought.

"What's he like?" Edie asked. "Old? Young? What?"

"About the same age as Dad, I suppose," Ali said. "And big. He had to use a seatbelt extender in the airplane."

"I don't care one whit about his size," Edie declared. "What I want to know is whether or not he's any good. Now what kind of attorney is he again? Not your divorce attorney," she added. "That's Myra somebody."

Ali wondered how it was Edie Larson could somehow play dumb while simultaneously and unerringly sniffing out Ali's every attempt at subterfuge.

"Not Myra, Helga Myerhoff," Ali corrected. "She was the one handling the divorce proceedings. Victor specializes in criminal defense."

"But why on earth would you need a criminal defense attorney?" Edie wanted to know. "Do the cops think you had something to do with Paul's death—that you're somehow responsible? How could you be? You were miles away at the time."

Ali remembered the pulsing, telltale glow from that long line of emergency lights that had lit up the desert floor as they streamed through the night toward the scene of the wreck.

Not nearly as many miles away as I should have been, Ali thought.

Victor hadn't wanted her to mention seeing those flashing lights in the course of giving Detectives Sims and Taylor her taped statement, but since they already knew what time she'd left Phoenix and since they already knew what time she'd checked into the hotel, that meant they also knew the approximate time she would have been passing Palm Springs. Consequently, it seemed pointless to skip over that part. The truth was, she *had* seen the flashing lights. She would have had to be blind not to, and lying about that in an official statement seemed both pointless and stupid.

"The cops probably do suspect me," Ali said, trying to deliver the words in a casual, offhand manner that she hoped would throw Edie off course. "But Victor says not to worry. It's just routine. That's what homicide detectives do. To begin with, they look at everyone. Then gradually they eliminate the ones who didn't do it until they arrive at whoever did."

"So you're saying for sure that Paul was murdered?" Edie asked.

Ali sighed. "Yes. When Victor and I left Indio, they hadn't yet released any details about the case because April hadn't been notified, but I'm sure she has been by now. If that's the case, the story is probably all over the airwaves. I was asleep, though, so I haven't had a chance to check."

The idea that the questioning was routine did nothing to calm Edie's outrage. "This is unbelievable!" she announced. "I should never have let you drive over there on your own. Never. The subject came up before you left. Dad said I should probably pack up and go along, but then I let you talk me out of it. Big mistake. There are times women need their mothers with them, Alison. This turns out to be one of them."

In the background Ali heard a door open and close. "Speak of the devil," Edie said. "Here's your father now. I'm in the office, Bob," she called to her husband. "Ali's on the phone. Come listen to this. You're not going to believe it."

Briefly Edie began to recount everything Ali had told her. Halfway through, though, the story came to an abrupt stop.

"My word!" Edie exclaimed. "I completely lost track of time. The first customers just pulled up, Ali. We have to go now. I'll call again later, but you take care of yourself. Don't let those turkeys push you around."

Once Ali put down the phone, she dozed for a little while, but by seven when she was wide awake, she called room service and ordered breakfast and newspapers. She managed to jump in and out of the shower before her breakfast tray showed up.

Sipping coffee, she went through the newspapers, where the homicide—yes, a Riverside Sheriff's Department spokesman actually used the H-word—of prominent television news executive Paul Grayson was front-page news. So, unfortunately, was Ali's picture, which turned out to be every bit as bad as Ali had predicted it would be. The caption stated: "Former L.A.-area news-caster Alison Reynolds, accompanied by noted defense attorney Victor Angeleri, leaves the Riverside County Sheriff's Substation in Indio after identifying the body of her slain husband, Paul Grayson."

Trying not to look at the tabloid-worthy photo, Ali turned her attention to the accompanying article. Despite the use of a banner headline and the expenditure of lots of front-page column inches, there was surprisingly little content, and hardly anything Ali hadn't already gleaned on her own.

> Today was supposed to be Paul Grayson's wedding day. Instead, the prospective groom is now a murder victim, having fallen victim to a bizarre kidnapping/murder scheme in which he was left bound and gagged in the trunk of a stolen vehicle that was abandoned on a railroad track near Palm Springs. The stolen vehicle was subsequently struck by a speeding freight train, killing Grayson on impact. An autopsy has been scheduled for later today.

> A joint homicide investigation by the Los Angeles Police Department and the Riverside County Sheriff's Department is attempting to establish the exact chain of events from the time Grayson abruptly departed a posh bachelor party being held in his honor to the time an eastbound Burlington Northern freight train slammed into the vehicle in which he had been imprisoned.

Ali scanned the next several paragraphs, which mostly contained information she had already learned. She slowed and read more carefully when she reached the part that discussed the ill-fated bachelor party at the Pink Swan.

"We were all at the Pink Swan having a good time," said bachelor party host and former NBC executive Jake Maxwell. "I remember someone saying there was a call for Paul. I believe he went outside to take it, and he never came back. I finally went outside looking for him and noticed his Porsche was missing from the parking lot. I just assumed he'd decided he'd had enough and gone home."

Early yesterday afternoon, Mr. Grayson's Porsche Carrera was found stripped and abandoned in an apartment parking lot in Banning. The Camry destroyed by the speeding train had been reported stolen earlier in the day from a vacant-lot private-vehicle sales location in Ventura. The Riverside Sheriff's Department is asking that anyone with information on either vehicle contact them immediately.

Mr. Grayson was in the process of divorcing his wife, former local television news personality Alison Reynolds. He was due at a hearing to finalize their divorce at 10 A.M. yesterday morning. It was his failure to appear in court that prompted his fiancée, April Gaddis, to contact LAPD's Missing Persons Unit, which immediately began conducting an investigation.

The story continued on page two, but Ali didn't bother following it. There was nothing new here. She tried two other papers with similar results—much the same story with no additional information and with equally bad photos of Alison Reynolds. Disgusted, Ali gave up, poured another cup of coffee, and turned on her computer. Once it booted up, she logged on and went to check out her new mail. Scanning the subject lines, she saw that three of them were addressed to Fred, the guy who had objected to the fact that Ali was divorcing her husband.

> Dear Fred,
> You are an ignorant asshole. I hope you die.

So much for reasoned discussion. That one was unsigned, and Ali simply deleted it.

> Dear Fred,
> You sound just like my first husband, and
> you know what? It's been years now and he
> still hasn't figured out how come I took the
> kids and left him. I tried to tell him his actions
> were pulling us apart, but he didn't want to
> hear it—so he didn't hear it. It was a struggle,
> but money isn't everything. I know the kids
> and I—two daughters and a son—are all
> better off.
>
> CONNIE IN MI

Dear Fred,
Let no man put asunder? God must have heard
what Fang did to Babe, and She smacked him a
good one. Maybe She'll smack you, too. Sounds
like you deserve it.

CASEY THE OLD BAT

Casey was someone who wrote in often. Usually Ali posted her comments, but this time they were a little too close to the "hope you die" one. Ali deleted Casey instead. As she was about to move on, a click announced a new e-mail, this one also addressed to Fred. But what caught Ali's attention was the sender's address, sugarloafmama.

Dear Fred,
I agree with you. Marriage vows are sacred, but
they need to be kept by both parties involved.
It reminds me of that old song, about Frankie
and Johnny. "He was her man but he done her
wrong." All I can say is, good riddance!

SUGARLOAFMAMA

Laughing, Ali posted Edie's comment. Anyone who lived in or around Sedona would know exactly who Sugarloafmama was. And the fact that Edie Larson held some reasonably strong opinions on any given subject, especially her former son-in-law, wouldn't be news, either.

*Google sent me here. I thought this was a health
care site. If I wanted advice to the lovelorn, I'd go
to Dear Abby. You guys should get a life.*

That one was unsigned and it went away. After that
Ali read a whole series of comments that were essentially notes of condolence to her. One in particular
stood out.

Dear Babe,
I understood exactly what you meant when you
said you didn't know what to feel and that you
couldn't cry. My divorce had been final for only
two weeks when my husband committed suicide.
He always said he would but I didn't believe him.
I needed him out of my life. He was into meth
and gambling both, and watching him destroy
himself was killing me. But I didn't mean for him
to die. For a long time I thought his death was my
fault. It took three years of therapy for me to come
to terms with what happened.

So please accept my condolences. I'm sure
you loved Fang once. According to my therapist, I
had to grieve not only for the man who was gone
but also for the man who never was—and for the
dream I once had about how our life together
would be. Grieving for the dream is as hard as
grieving for the person. Don't be afraid to seek
help if you think you need it. But it's hard work.
Harder than anything I've ever done.

I've been a cutloose fan for a long time.
Through the months I know you've focused a

lot of your anger on Twink even more so than on Fang. I understand that, as far as you're concerned, Twink is "the other woman," but I also suspect that she's much younger than you are and not nearly as smart. She isn't going to have the emotional resources you have to deal with this tragedy. Try to remember that her dreams are in ashes today, too, right along with yours.

Since your divorce from Fang wasn't final when his death occurred, I expect that you and Twink will find your lives intertwined in unexpected ways. I hope you can find it in your heart to be kind to her and to her innocent baby as well.

Remember, God will see to it that you reap what you sow.

PHYLLIS IN KNOXVILLE

Ali was in tears by the time she finished reading Phyllis's note. There was so much hard-won wisdom in the words and so much caring that it took Ali's breath away. She posted the note in the comments section and then sent Phyllis a personal response.

Dear Phyllis,
Thank you for writing. Thank you for your kindness—for knowing what I was feeling and giving me comfort; for giving me much needed guidance when I was in danger of losing my way.

BABE

Several of the other notes were in the same vein. Ali responded to them all, but the one from Phyllis was the only one she posted. That was the one that said it all and said it best. When her cell phone rang a little later, she expected the caller to be one of her parents or maybe even Chris. She didn't expect to hear the voice of Dave Holman—Yavapai County homicide detective Dave Holman.

"I just talked to your mom," Dave said grimly. "Is it true? Do the cops out in L.A. think you're involved in Paul's murder?"

In the years before Sedona had built its own high school, kids from Sedona had been bused to Mingus Mountain High School in Cottonwood. Dave Holman had been a tall skinny kid a year ahead of Ali in school. After graduation, he had joined the Marines. He went to college later, studying criminal justice. He was both a detective in the sheriff's department and a captain in the Marine Reserves who had served two tours of duty in Iraq. He was also a much-valued breakfast regular at Bob and Edie Larson's Sugar Loaf Café.

Ali felt an initial stab of resentment that her parents had spilled the beans about what was going on in her life. Then she remembered her blog. Maybe Dave read cutlooseblog.com the same way Ali's mother did. Maybe that was where he was getting his information—everything but her phone number, that is.

Why was it I wanted to have a blog? Ali asked herself.

"They didn't come right out and say so," Ali replied. "Not in so many words."

"What words?" Dave asked. "Tell me exactly what was said."

"They took my statement," Ali said.

"With your attorney present, this Angel guy?"

Obviously Edie had given Dave a complete briefing on Ali's conversation with her.

"Angeleri," Ali corrected. "Victor Angeleri, and yes, he was there."

"Edie says you told them about driving past the crash site, seeing the emergency vehicles, all that?"

"I had to," Ali said. "It's the truth. I could see those lights from miles away. Coming past Palm Springs at that time of night, I couldn't not see them."

"Great," Dave muttered. "What else did they have to say?"

"I don't know. They asked a bunch of questions. I answered them. End of story."

"What did they say when the interview was over?"

"What do you mean?" Ali asked. "You mean, like, did they say good-bye?"

"No, I mean like, 'Don't leave the state without letting us know.'"

Ali paused. "Well, yes," she said at length. "I suppose they did mention something to that effect. They told me they'd be pursuing all possible leads but it might be best if I stayed around L.A. for a while. I told them that was fine. That I had planned to be here several more days. They hinted it might take a little longer than that for them to get all their ducks in a row."

"I'll just bet," Dave said. "Well, it doesn't matter. I'm glad your mother is on her way."

"Mom is coming here—to L.A.?"

"Yes. Edie Larson is riding to the rescue. Didn't she tell you?"

"No," Ali said. "As a matter of fact she didn't. I'll call and tell her not to come."

"That's probably why she didn't mention it to you, and by now it's too late, because she's already on her way. I may show up, too," Dave added. "I came to Lake Havasu to see the kids this weekend, which means I'm only four and a half hours away."

Ali knew that since Dave's ex-wife and her new husband had taken the children and moved to Lake Havasu City, Dave had spent at least one weekend a month going there to see them.

"Really, Dave," she told him. "That's not necessary. What about your kids?"

"What about them? I already did what Rich wanted me to do this weekend—which was to get him signed up for his learner's permit. As for Cassie and Crystal? They'll be glad to have me out of their hair. Spending weekends with me is more of a hassle for my daughters than it is anything else. I'm not nearly cool enough to suit them."

"But it makes no sense for both you and Mom to drop everything and come running to California," Ali argued. "I'm sure this is no big deal."

"No big deal?" Dave repeated. "Are you kidding? Being accused of murder is always a big deal, even if you end up getting off. Ask O. J. Simpson. Ask Robert Blake. And since you obviously don't want me to do this for you, let's just say I'm doing it for your folks—for your mom. This is my cell phone, by the way," he added. "Feel free to call me on it anytime if you need to."

The truth of the matter was, Ali still had Dave's cell phone number stored in her phone. She had needed his help once, desperately, when the abusive husband of one of her cutloose fans had come looking for Ali. But there was no way she was going to admit that to him, especially not right then.

"I still think this is silly," she said.

"Everybody's entitled to his or her opinion," Dave returned. "I don't have enough available cell phone minutes to waste time arguing about it."

"All right," Ali said, capitulating. "You know where to come?"

"Edie gave me the address. Rich is putting it into MapQuest right now. Unfortunately my Nissan Sentra doesn't come equipped with the fancy-schmancy GPS you have in your Cayenne. I can't leave until a little later, but I'll be there."

He hung up. Ali was still holding the phone in her hand when it rang again. "Ali?"

Helga's near-baritone usually made people think they were talking to a man. Ali knew better. "What's up?" Ali asked.

"Are you decent?"

"Not exactly."

"Get that way," Helga ordered, "and then meet us downstairs."

"Us?"

"Victor and me," Helga said. "We have an appointment with Ted Grantham half an hour from now."

"With Ted?" Ali asked. "What for?"

"With Ted and with Les Jordan," Helga replied.

"Who's Les Jordan?"

"Paul Grayson's estate planning attorney."

Far be it for Paul to have one attorney when he could have two, Ali thought. Then she realized she had no room to talk.

"Why are we meeting him?" she asked.

"For a reading of the will."

"Now?" Ali wanted to know. "Don't people usually read wills after funerals instead of before?"

"Under normal circumstances that's true," Helga said. "But these circumstances are far from normal. Meet us downstairs in fifteen minutes."

{ CHAPTER 5 }

Victor and Helga arrived together in Victor's silver Lincoln Town Car. When Ali looked inside the vehicle, she could see that Victor took up more than half of the front seat, with the steering wheel grazing his ample belly. Helga, on the other hand, was so tiny that once Ali settled into the backseat, the top of the diminutive attorney's hairdo didn't clear the headrest.

"I'm not sure why we're doing this in such an unseemly hurry," Ali said, once her seat belt was fastened. "Yesterday we found out Paul was dead. Today's the day he and April were supposed to get married. Couldn't we wait a day or two and give the poor woman a chance to adjust?"

"We're doing it now because we need to," Victor

said. "Because if the cops are going to pin a murder-for-profit motive on you, we need to know whether or not it will fly, and it may, especially if you're still a beneficiary under the will. The cops will naturally expect that the will won't be read until after the funeral, and they know the funeral can't take place until after the coroner releases the body—sometime next week. In other words, reading the will now gives us an investigational leg up for at least the next several days."

"We're also reading it now because Ted Grantham is a spineless wuss," Helga observed. "When I called and suggested reading the will today, he practically fell all over himself saying yes. He even suggested we go to the house to do it. He said he'd call Les Jordan and April and set it up."

Ali was dismayed. "We're going to the house on Robert Lane?" she asked. "Couldn't we do this somewhere else—anywhere else? Why would Grantham suggest such a thing? Why would you agree to it?"

"Because evidently he doesn't think April's in any condition to go elsewhere," Helga said. "I think he also agreed to reading the will today because he's nervous. His divorce case is in the toilet, but he still wants to be paid. Grantham may not have drafted the new will, but I'm guessing he knows the terms. He hasn't come right out and said so—that would be a breach of client privilege—but from the way he's acting, I'm guessing the new will has been drafted without being put into effect."

"And I'm still the main beneficiary?"

"Right," Helga answered. "So Grantham is making nice with us because he thinks you'll be the one settling Paul's estate—as well as paying any outstanding bills."

"He's doing this because he's buttering us up?"

"Buttering *you* up," Helga corrected. "He also said something about preserving community assets. I think he's worried about handing things off to you before any of those assets has a chance to disappear. If that were to happen, he's concerned he might somehow end up being held responsible."

"What do you mean disappear?" Ali asked.

"You've never had the pleasure of meeting April Gaddis," Helga said with a disdainful sniff. "Ted has met her, and so have I. Prior to meeting your husband and signing on for what she thought would be a very luxurious free ride, her greatest ambition was to become a Pilates instructor someday. She's gorgeous but not exactly the brightest bulb I ever met. The same goes for some of the bodybuilding pals she likes to hang out with. I wouldn't call them the salt of the earth, either. April's bachelorette party the other night was wild enough that the cops had to be summoned to quiet things down—and that's with her about to give birth.

"Ted's worried that when some of the more disreputable wedding guests who've been staying at the house pack up to go home, some of Paul's precious objets d'art might end up going home with them. Grantham is lobbying for you to demand a full inventory of the contents of the Robert Lane house—an immediate full inventory."

"In other words," Ali said, "Ted's rooting for the old will over the new one because he expects to hand the whole mess over to me and maybe get paid faster besides. But if the old will is still in effect and I'm the primary beneficiary, doesn't that give me a clear motive for wanting Paul dead? Doesn't it make me look that much worse to the cops?"

"That just about covers it," Victor agreed. "What's good for Ted could be bad for us."

"I still don't like the fact that we're having the will read now," Ali said after a pause. "It seems rude and pushy."

They had come to a stop at a light on Sunset. Victor sought Ali's eyes in the rearview mirror. "It probably is rude and pushy," he agreed. "But let me remind you, this is a homicide investigation, Ali—possibly even capital murder. With your life at stake, you by God better believe we're going to be pushy."

"All right," Ali conceded finally. "Fair enough."

Robert Lane was only a few blocks long and sat on top of a steep hill just up from Sunset Boulevard; it was a winding, narrow, and supposedly two-way street. Whenever Paul and Ali had thrown parties—which they had done often—they had rented the parking lot from a neighboring church down on Sunset and then hired one of the local parking valet firms to ferry guests' cars up and down the hill.

Since the wedding and reception had both been scheduled to take place at the house, Ali assumed the parking arrangements would have been canceled once the wedding was called off. The sides of the street were full of illegally parked vehicles, most of them bearing media insignia. When Victor pulled up to the gate, Ali was surprised to see that it was wide open. She was even more surprised to see the parking valets very much in evidence although most of the newsies had chosen to disregard the valet parking option. So did Victor.

"Keep your cool, Ali," he advised as he turned in at the gate. He maneuvered his Lincoln into a narrow parking place between a catering truck—if the wedding had been canceled, why a catering truck?—and an enormous RV garishly painted an overall red and blue plaid pattern. On the side was a picture of a muscle-bound, bare-chested man wearing little more than a kilt. Beside him, printed in huge gold letters, were the words TEAM MCLAUGHLIN. SUMO SUDOKU.

Ali had a passing knowledge of sudoku. In fact, the waitresses at the Sugar Loaf had become sudoku addicts and experts, spending their break times working the puzzles in discarded newspapers left behind by customers who weren't so afflicted.

Puzzles of any kind had never really appealed to Ali, but she had learned enough to understand that sudoku was a game of logic played on a square containing eighty-one boxes divided into nine smaller squares. It was similar to a crossword puzzle only with numbers rather than words. The object was to fill in all horizontal and vertical lines with the numbers one through nine without ever having the same number appear twice in any of the lines. Each of the smaller boxes was also supposed to contain the numbers one through nine with no repetition. Ali assumed that Sumo Sudoku was more of the same, only bigger.

"Your husband's death is a big story, and everybody is covering it," Victor cautioned. "That means there may be reporters outside the door. So when we get out of the vehicle to go inside, try to keep quiet. I don't want any off-the-cuff remarks from anybody, you included, Helga," he added.

With Ali's attention focused on the garishly painted truck, she almost missed the group of reporters bearing down on them as Ted Grantham hustled out of the house to usher them inside. "Right this way," he said hurriedly. "Les isn't here yet. He called to say he's tied up in traffic. April should be down in a few minutes."

Down from what used to be my *room,* Ali thought, but she said nothing.

"Sorry about all the uproar," Ted commented, leading them toward the front door, where a hand-lettered DO NOT DISTURB sign had been posted over the doorbell. "But the film crew was already scheduled to be here today as part of the festivities," he continued. "Since this is the only day they *can* be here, April decided to go ahead with the shoot after all. Even with Paul gone, she thinks once the program is in the can there's a chance they'll still be able to get it on the air—maybe on one of those reality shows."

"What shoot?" Helga asked.

"The Sumo Sudoku shoot," Ted answered. "Surely you've heard of Sumo Sudoku. It's Paul's latest brainchild. April's, too, for that matter. It's all the rage around here and supposedly the next big thing. You play it with rocks. When Tracy McLaughlin of Team McLaughlin takes the RV down to the beach and sets up a match there, it's amazing. People line up to play; they're even willing to fork over good money for the privilege."

Only half listening to Ted, Ali stepped through the double doors with their elegant frosted glass and into the spacious foyer. It was a strange experience. This light-washed entryway with its hardwood floor and antique credenza had once been part of her home. Most of the house had been decorated in accordance with Paul's unrelentingly modern sensibility. In the face of all that brass and glass, Ali had gravitated to the one exception—a beautifully wrought, bird's-eye maple credenza that had occupied the place of honor in the entryway. She had loved the slightly curved lines of the piece and complex patterns in the grain of the wood. In a way, the credenza had seemed almost as much of an interloper in Paul's house as Ali herself had been.

Now the credenza was covered with a collection of fragrant condolence bouquets, all of them complete with unopened envelopes from various senders. At least one of the vases had been carelessly deposited on the polished wood, leaving behind a distinct and indelible water mark. Seeing the stain saddened Ali. She made a halfhearted effort to rub it out but it didn't go away. It would take someone wiser in the ways of cleaning to make the offending moisture ring disappear.

With no one paying any attention to her, Ali ventured a few steps into the living room. In anticipation of the wedding, most of the furniture had been removed—replaced by a dozen or so rows of cloth-covered banquet-style chairs arranged so they faced a wooden arch at one end of the room. On either side of the arch stood ranks of candles and immense baskets of flowers—an avant-garde mix of traditional and fragrant lilies punctuated with an occasional bird-of-paradise.

Ali wasn't the least bit surprised by this somewhat odd combination. Bird-of-paradise wasn't exactly commonplace in bridal floral arrangements, but Paul had always preferred it to any other flower. He would insist on sending it on occasions when other people—Ali included—would have preferred roses or gladiolas or even snapdragons. The oddly angular buds with their comical topknots and brilliant colors had never spoken to Ali the way they had to him.

The same could be said of Paul's choices in furniture—unabashedly modern and not especially comfortable—and art. On this early Saturday morning, with most of the furniture removed in honor of a wedding that would never happen, only the artwork remained. The big splashy original oil canvases had bold colors and plenty of panache. Ali knew the paintings came with top gallery pedigrees and spectacular price tags. What they lacked was heart.

Just like the rest of the house, Ali thought. No wonder she had never felt at home here. If it hadn't been for Elvira Jimenez doing her cooking magic in the kitchen, the house on Robert Lane could just as well have been a museum of modern art.

The far wall of the living room was lined with French doors that led out onto a spacious terrace. Through the open doors, Ali saw the terrace was stocked with a dozen or so linen-covered cocktail tables and even more chairs. Empty buffet tables, chafing dishes at the ready, were situated at both ends of the terrace. Again, Ali wasn't surprised that Paul would have selected this spot as the site of his now-canceled wedding reception. Paul had always loved entertaining on the lavish terrace with its unobstructed if sometimes smog-obscured view of the city. Ali had usually gravitated toward the smaller and more private tree-and-bougainvillea-lined patio out back by the pool house.

With the three attorneys settled in the library in a

low-voiced huddle, Ali wandered out onto the terrace. The grassy lawn below the stone balustrade was a bee-hive of activity. Someone was using a handheld dispenser to lay out a complicated pattern of white chalk lines on Paul's carefully tended grass. Ali looked around for Jesus Sanchez, Paul's longtime gardener. He had always taken great pride in the fact that his grass could have been plunked down on the eighteenth green of any self-respecting golf course without anyone knowing the difference. Ali more than half expected Jesus to appear out of nowhere, bellowing a loud objection to the chalk-spreader's desecration.

Moments later Jesus did in fact appear around the corner of the house above and behind Ali, but he wasn't making any kind of fuss about the chalk on his grass lawn. Instead, he was totally occupied by two young men who were pushing a pair of heavily laden wheel-barrows loaded with perfectly round rocks down the steep path that led from the back of the house to the lawn below.

As one of the men made the corner, the wheelbarrow wobbled in his hands. The next thing Ali knew, the load of rocks came spilling down the hill and onto the flag-stone terrace. Some of them bounced almost head high while one of them smashed to pieces, sending shards of granite flying in every direction. One needlelike piece seemed headed directly for Ali's throat. It missed her by an inch. Seconds later, a man vaulted off the path and over the rail, landing on the terrace next to her.

"Are you all right?"

Ali was shaken but unhurt. "I'm fine," she said.

Nodding, the angry man turned back to the frightened workman who was still clinging to the handles of his empty wheelbarrow.

"You stupid jerk! Don't you know how to do anything? You could have killed this poor woman!"

Only then did Ali recognize him. The man doing the yelling had to be Tracy McLaughlin, the same tall blond guy pictured on the RV. The big difference was that now he wore regular khakis rather than a kilt.

"Are you sure you're all right?" he asked Ali again. "It's a good thing that eight broke into a million pieces. Otherwise it might have taken your head right off. I'm not surprised, though. The kind of piss-poor help we're having to put up with here today . . ." He shook his head in disgust. "Come get these, will you?" he shouted up at the men waiting on the path. "And then go back to the truck. Thank God I have a spare eight there. It's got a crack in it, but it'll have to do."

As the one man came to collect his scattered load, the other made his way down to the grass. "Don't put them there, you stupid asshole," Tracy shouted at him. "Don't you know anything? Those are the fours. They belong on this side."

As the man hefted the rocks out of another wheelbarrow and onto the ground, the truth about Sumo Sudoku finally came home to Ali. When Ted had said it was played with rocks, Ali had envisioned something the size of marbles. These smooth, round hunks of granite were more like boulders, with large numbers chiseled into the surface. From the size and obvious weight of the "fours," Ali could only guess how much damage the stray eight might have done had it hit her full on.

Ali was still shaken from her near miss when she

saw a young woman, blond and very pregnant, emerge from the living room. She walked over to the debris field left by the broken rock and kicked at some of it. "What's this?" she wanted to know.

Helga had said April Gaddis was gorgeous, and that was true. Even without makeup and with her hair in disarray, she was a fine-featured beauty except for her eyes. They were red and puffy from a combination of weeping and lack of sleep. And she was pregnant enough that the silk robe she wore didn't quite cover her expanded middle. She was beautiful but utterly distraught and very, very young.

"One of my rocks," Tracy explained. "That cretin up there didn't know how to work a friggin' wheelbarrow. He lost his whole load and it came crashing down on the terrace here. It's a wonder he didn't kill this lady. A miracle really."

As the workman in question scurried to load the remaining rocks back into his wheelbarrow, April looked at Ali uncertainly.

"What are you doing here?" April asked. At least she didn't try to pretend that she didn't know who Ali was.

"The lawyers," Ali said, quickly forgetting her near miss with the exploding rock. "We're supposed to be meeting with the lawyers this morning in the library."

April shrugged. "I'm not in any condition to deal with this stuff right now. All I was trying to do was sneak down and get some breakfast from the buffet, but there are way too many workmen here already. I had no idea the crew would be this big."

Ali had sometimes imagined how she would react in what she had thought was the unlikely event she would ever come face-to-face with April Gaddis, her rival. Ali had scripted any number of biting remarks, but faced with the young woman and seeing her obvious desolation, Ali forgot all of them. Instead, Ali tried to focus on the homespun wisdom passed along to her in the e-mail from Phyllis in Knoxville.

"I'm sorry we're meeting like this, April," Ali said kindly. "I'm sorry for your loss."

Ali's words seemed to sap all of the young woman's strength. April staggered over to a nearby table, where she sank onto a chair and made a halfhearted attempt to smooth her hair.

"No one told me *you'd* be coming," she said accusingly.

"Ted Grantham is the one who set up the meeting," Ali returned. "He should have told you."

"He didn't." April seemed close to tears.

"I'm sorry," Ali said.

April probably could have handled a fight, but she was unable to cope with kindness. Her lips trembled, her face crumpled. Burying her head in her hands, she began to sob.

"I can't believe any of this is happening," she said despondently. "This was supposed to be my wedding day. I can't believe Paul is gone, just like that—with no warning at all. Instead of our wedding guests, the house is full of lawyers who are here about his will. Paul's *will*, for God's sake! What am I going to do without him? How will I manage? What'll happen to me? What'll happen to my baby?"

April's unbridled grief over losing Paul struck Ali as utterly raw and real—and refreshingly different from her own conflicted emotions. Learning about Paul's death—seeing him dead—had left Ali more empty than sad. Having him dead made her own life far less complicated. She hadn't cried. In fact, she hadn't shed a single tear, not even in the coroner's office. For that she felt guilty. In a way, being a party to April Gaddis's uncompromising despair made Ali feel better. She was relieved to know that Paul's sudden death meant something to someone—even if that person was the one who had unceremoniously booted Ali out of her home and out of her marriage.

And where were April's friends? Why was she here all alone? Without thinking about it, Ali sat down next to the grieving woman, laying a compassionate hand on her shoulder. What this very pregnant twenty-five-year-old was facing now was territory Ali Reynolds knew all too well. She had been there once, too, only she had been a few years younger than April when it had happened to her.

Ali had been a happily married twenty-two-year-old and pregnant with Chris when her first husband, Dean Reynolds, had been diagnosed with glioblastoma and died within months. Ali knew what it meant to be expecting a baby who would most likely be and indeed was a fatherless child on the day he was born. She remembered lying awake at night, pregnant, with her back hurting, and with the baby hurtling around inside her womb, and asking those very same questions over and over: What will become of us? How can I raise this baby on my own? Why is this happening to me?

During those dark, sleepless nights she hadn't known that she would be able to make it; that despite being a single mother she'd somehow manage to go back to school to finish her education and then go on to have a life and career that most people would have thought of as charmed. Back in that terrible time, there had been no easy answers for her, and she didn't try to pass along any easy answers to April Gaddis, either.

"You'll manage," Ali said, patting the weeping woman on the shoulder. "Being a single mother is tough. There are times when the baby is crying and the responsibility is all on your shoulders and you'll think you won't be able to live through one more day, but you will. There are times you'll question God and times when you'll rail at Him. But some day, on a bright fall afternoon, you'll be standing on the sidelines of a soccer field cheering like mad when that baby of yours kicks his first goal. That's when you'll know God was right; that's when you'll know everything you went through was worth it."

April raised her head. Her bleak eyes met Ali's. "But the divorce didn't go through," she said. "Paul and I weren't even married. What if he left me out of his will? He said he was going to rewrite it. He told me he had, but what if he didn't? Where will the baby and I live? What am I going to *do*? What?"

Ali could see that April's grief had her operating on a very short loop. "That's why we both have attorneys," Ali counseled gently. "I'm sure that's what they're doing right now—they're inside sorting things out."

"But I don't even have an attorney," April said. "I never thought I needed one."

Oh, honey lamb, Ali thought, *if you were messing around with Paul Grayson, how wrong you were!*

"It's going to be okay," Ali said with more conviction than she felt.

"Are you sure?" April asked.

Ali nodded. "Now what about you? You look a little queasy. You said you were looking for something to eat?"

Faced with a crisis, Ali automatically reverted to the coping skills she had learned at her mother's knee. In the Edie Larson school of crisis management there was nothing so bad that it couldn't be improved by the application of some well-prepared food served with equal amounts of tender loving care and judicious advice.

April nodded. "I called down to the kitchen, but no one answered. The cook's probably out overseeing the caterers for the film crew."

Ali stood up. "Someone in your condition shouldn't be running on empty. Let me go ask Elvira to fix you something. An omelet, maybe? Elvira's huevos rancheros are wonderful, but probably not for someone as pregnant as you are."

"Elvira doesn't work here anymore," April said. "She quit, or else Paul fired her. I'm not sure which."

Ali was surprised to hear Elvira was gone—surprised and sorry, both. "But you do have a cook," Ali confirmed.

April nodded.

"Why don't I go find her," Ali offered. "What's her name?"

"We've gone through half a dozen cooks since that first one left," April said. "Sorry. I don't know her name."

"What would you like then?"

"Toast," April said uncertainly. "And maybe some orange juice."

"How about some bacon?"

"Oh, no. I don't eat anything that had a face. I'm a vegan."

That was, of course, utterly predictable. "Whole wheat?" Ali asked.

"Yes, please. With marmalade. And coffee. Have her make me a latte—a vanilla latte."

Ali wasn't sure a dose of caffeine was in the baby's best interests, but she set off for the kitchen without saying anything. On the way she caught a glimpse of Ted Grantham, Victor Angeleri, and Helga Myerhoff still huddled in the library, still conferring. In the spacious kitchen, Ali found a heavyset black woman standing in front of the stainless steel sinks and working her way through a mountain of dirty dishes.

"The breakfast buffet's out by the pool house," she said impatiently. "That's where the film crew is. There's food and coffee out there. Help yourself."

She sounded exasperated, overworked, and underappreciated if not underpaid. Having another stranger wander into her kitchen was more than she could handle.

"This is for April—for Ms. Gaddis," Ali explained. "She asked me if you could make her some toast— whole wheat toast with marmalade, orange juice, and a vanilla latte."

The woman shook excess water off her hands and then dried them on a tea towel. "Very well," she said with a curt nod. "Do you want to wait here for it or should I bring it to her?"

"It might be best if you brought it," Ali said. "We're out on the terrace."

"You want some coffee, too?"

"Yes, thank you," Ali said. "That would be nice."

Ali returned to the terrace to find April sitting exactly where Ali had left her. She seemed to be absorbed in watching the ongoing rock-hauling and arranging process down below, but when Ali sat down next to her, she realized April was really staring off into space, seeing nothing.

"Breakfast's on its way," Ali said.

April nodded without answering.

"So when's the baby due?" Ali asked. She hoped that drawing April into a conversation might help shake her out of her solitary reverie and back into the present.

"Two weeks," she said. "Paul wanted to go to the condo in Aspen on our honeymoon, but my ob-gyn said I shouldn't fly this close to my due date. We were going to drive over to Vegas instead."

"Do you know if it's a boy or a girl?"

"A girl. Paul wanted to name her Sonia Marie. I don't like that name much," April added, "but I guess I'll use it anyway. I wanted something a little more modern. You know—like Hermione from Harry Potter."

To Ali's way of thinking, Sonia Marie was a better bet than Hermione any day, but Paul was gone now. Soon enough April would realize that, when it came to her child, she was the one who would be making the decisions—all of them. By virtue of being run over by a freight train, Paul Grayson no longer had any effective say in the matter.

"Breakfast is coming," Ali said. "It'll be right out."

"Thank you," April said. Then, after a pause she added, "Thank you for being so nice to me."

You have a lady named Phyllis to thank for that, Ali thought. *Someone you've never met and most likely never will.*

She said, "This is a very tough situation, and we'll probably have to work together to sort it all out. It'll be better for all concerned if we can be civil to each other."

April nodded. "Did the cops tell you Paul was murdered?"

"Yes."

"Who would do such a thing?" April asked as the tears started up again. "I just can't imagine it. How could they be so cold-blooded as to put him on the train tracks and just leave him there to die?"

"I can't imagine that, either," Ali said. And it was true. The idea was as unfathomable for her as it was for April.

"They think whoever did it left him there and then escaped by walking down the train tracks," April continued. "That's why they didn't find any footprints at the scene. They must have planned it that way so there wouldn't be any evidence. They think the killer had an accomplice who met him somewhere down the tracks, and that's how he got away. They said he was probably still in the area when Paul died. I guess the engine on the Camry was still warm when the cops got there. Can you imagine doing something like that and then standing around waiting for it to happen?"

April's words chilled Ali. If the killer had been somewhere nearby when the crash occurred, then he was probably still there when the emergency vehicles were dispatched to the scene as well—at the same time Ali herself was driving past on the freeway.

That meant the cops would go looking for someone who might have given the escaping killer a ride. That also meant Detectives Sims and Taylor wouldn't have far to look, especially if the old will was still in effect. They'd come after Ali—with a vengeance.

As someone with the three necessary ingredients—motive, opportunity, and an unidentified accomplice—Ali would be exactly what the detectives wanted and needed, a prime suspect.

{ CHAPTER 6 }

It turned out April was hungry enough that one order of toast and marmalade wasn't enough to do the job. Ali went back to the kitchen for a second helping. When she returned with it, she was surprised to find a camera crew had arrived. Someone was sweeping up the broken rock, and others were setting up cameras on the side of the terrace, where the city of L.A. would serve as a backdrop. She returned to the table just as Tracy McLaughlin came jogging up the stairs and back onto the terrace.

Earlier, when he'd been giving grief to the grounds-keepers, he'd been clad in a T-shirt and a pair of khaki Bermuda shorts. Now he was dressed in what looked like the same kilt he'd worn for the RV mural. Tucked under one arm, like a football, was a ball of granite—a four, Ali estimated. Nodding briefly in April's direction, he marched over to the camera crew. He put the ball down on the flagstone terrace. When he straightened, he brushed a long lock of blond hair off his forehead and then stopped to confer with a member of the crew. Meanwhile, the ball of granite set off on its own and rolled drunkenly across the terrace. It came to rest near the leg of Ali's chair. A five-inch-tall numeral 3 had been sandblasted into its otherwise smooth surface. Having it roll in her direction seemed far less dangerous than having it bounce.

Leaving the camera crew, McLaughlin hurried over to retrieve it. "Sorry about that," he said.

"This is Tracy," April said to Ali. To Tracy she added, "And this is Ali."

No last names were mentioned or seemed to be necessary.

"Glad to meet you," Ali said.

He nodded. "Same here."

Just then a sweet young thing, a Hispanic woman in a very short skirt and very high heels, came through the French doors from the living room. Ali recognized her as a former intern from the station, although she couldn't remember the name. She wore a lapel mic and was dressed in a business suit—interviewer rather than intern attire. Obviously her career had taken an upward swing since Ali had last seen her. As she headed for the camera crew, so did Tracy.

"Now, if you'll excuse me," he said. Grabbing his ball, he hurried after her, smoothing his unruly hair as he went. Something about seeing the woman seemed to penetrate April's fog and she suddenly realized that, of all the people on the terrace, she was the only one wearing a robe.

Abruptly, she pushed her chair away from the table. "I've got to go get dressed," she said.

Since no one had come to summon Ali, she stayed where she was. A few seconds later, Tracy McLaughlin, still holding his granite ball, and Sandy Quijada—she announced her name at the beginning of the inter-view—stepped in front of the camera for an old-fashioned stand-up.

"This is Tracy McLaughlin," Sandy said, smiling engagingly into the camera. "You're generally credited with inventing Sumo Sudoku. Do you mind telling us how that all came about?"

"Just because someone is strong doesn't mean he's stupid," Tracy told her. "It's one of the oldest clichés in the book. I mean, how many times have you heard the words 'dumb as an ox'? If you're a jock, people auto-matically assume you're also a dolt. Sumo Sudoku is a game that mixes brains and brawn."

"How?" Sandy asked.

Not exactly insightful, Ali thought.

"Sudoku is a game of logic," Tracy replied. "Regular sudoku is usually played with a paper and pencil. Or a pen if you're very good."

"Like a crossword puzzle," Sandy supplied.

"Right," Tracy said. "Only with numbers instead of words. It's done on a square layout of eighty-one squares arranged in a nine-by-nine matrix. Numbers from one to nine are placed in the squares so that all values occur without repetition in each horizontal line, in each verti-

WEB OF EVIL 93

cal line, and in each of the nine three-by-three submatrices that fit within the nine-by-nine square."

Sandy frowned slightly, as though the word "submatrices" was leaving her in the dust. "So how is Sumo Sudoku different?"

Not a dumb blonde, Ali thought. *But dumb nevertheless.*

"For one thing, it's played outdoors," Tracy explained patiently. "Instead of using paper, we use grass or sand or even gravel. It has to be played on level ground so the numbers stay wherever they're placed. And instead of using a pencil to fill in the numbers, we use rocks like this." He hefted the granite ball into the air and held it up to the camera so that the sandblasted number 3 was showing.

"This is a number three rock. It weighs thirty pounds. The number one rocks weigh ten pounds. The number nine rocks weigh ninety pounds."

"That's a lot of rocks," Sandy marveled.

Tracy nodded. "It is," he agreed. "The total weight of the playing pieces is four thousand fifty pounds. Not exactly your grandfather's game of checkers."

"I'll say." Sandy beamed.

"So when we set up for a game, the grid is made up of individual squares that are two feet on each side, so a full layout is eighteen feet per side. As I said, the terrain should be flat enough to prevent placed markers from rolling on their own, but it may be flat or sloped, grassy or sandy—slightly damp sand is better than dry. Like golf, you must play the terrain as well as the basic game."

"Here you're going to play on grass?" Sandy asked.

If Tracy McLaughlin had a sense of humor, it wasn't

apparent in the dead seriousness of his responses. "That's right. The game is prepared by placing all the markers ten feet from the edge of the grid. The judges will place the starting pieces in position. They are marked with an International Orange adhesive tag and may not be moved for the duration of the round. The remainder of the pieces will remain untouched and on the sidelines until the starter's signal. Markers may be moved at will during the round, but doing so more than once will slow the competitor. Markers may be carried or rolled. Speed is essential. So is accuracy."

Listening to him drone on, outlining the rules, it occurred to Ali that she was listening to an engineer masquerading as a bodybuilder. Sandy's attention seemed to be wandering, too.

"So how will today's match work?"

"What's all this?" Victor Angeleri demanded. His sotto voce greeting to Ali provoked an angry frown and a shushing motion from a woman on the sidelines, one with more tattoos and piercings than clothing.

Ali rose to her feet and hurried inside with her attorney on her heels. "Mr. McLaughlin is outlining the rules for Sumo Sudoku," she said, once in the living room. "It's supposed to be the next big thing."

Victor stopped and looked back out on the terrace. "Really? Next to what?"

"Beach volleyball, for all I know," Ali answered. "But from what I'm hearing, I'm guessing the world is safe from Sumo Sudoku. What about the will?"

"Les just got here," Victor told her. "It's time."

Victor ushered her into Paul's study—what used to be Paul's study. An unfamiliar man was seated behind

Paul's ultramodern mirrored glass and stainless steel desk. He rose when Ali entered the room. "Les Jordan," he said. "You must be Ms. Reynolds."

Ali nodded.

"Sorry to be meeting under such unfortunate circumstances."

Ali nodded again. She looked around. Usually there were only three extra chairs in the room—two captain's chairs and a leather sling-backed contraption that was supposedly ergonomically superior to any other chair in the house. It was also Ali's least favorite. Helga was seated next to the wall in that one. It would probably soon be Helga's least favorite as well since her feet barely touched the floor. But today, with four lawyers already present, three extra swivel chairs from the game table in the family room had been crammed into the study as well.

Ali took one of those while Victor and Ted Grantham settled into the two captain's chairs. "I expect Ms. Gaddis should be joining us any moment," Mr. Jordan said seriously. "If you don't mind waiting . . ."

It wasn't lost on Ali that, while they waited for April to put in her appearance, Ali was sitting in a roomful of attorneys, all of them chalking up billable hours at an astonishing rate.

And it's all Paul's fault, she thought. *If he hadn't gone and gotten himself killed, if he'd tended to business, if he'd kept his pants zipped . . .*

"Would you care for some coffee?" Mr. Jordan asked.

There was something about being in her former home and being offered coffee by a visitor, especially a visiting attorney, that rubbed Ali the wrong way. "No thanks," she said. "April and I had coffee together out on the terrace a few minutes ago."

It was worth the price of admission—whatever that might be—to see four attorneys watching her in drop-jawed amazement. Before any of them replied, however, two newcomers showed up in the library doorway. One was a relatively attractive woman of indeterminate age. Her face was a tight-skinned mask that spoke of too many dollars spent on a high-priced plastic surgeon. Ali recognized the type—a Hollywood socialite wife—or more likely ex-wife—with more nerve than money. The bow tie–wearing man at the woman's side was, Ali realized at once, yet another attorney—making the grand total five in all. Five too many.

"Good morning, Mrs. Ragsdale," Les Jordan said smoothly, rising to his feet. "Come in, please. I didn't realize you would be here or that you'd be bringing someone with you. I'll send out for more chairs."

"We'll only need one," the woman said. "My daughter won't be attending this meeting after all. She's not feeling up to it."

"Well then," Les said, "with all due respect, you probably shouldn't be here, either, Mrs. Ragsdale. Client confidentiality rules and all that."

Dismissing him with a look, Mrs. Ragsdale turned away from Les Jordan and addressed the other people in the room. "My name's Monique Ragsdale," she said. "April Gaddis is my daughter. And this," she added, indicating the man beside her, "is Harlan Anderson. I've retained him to be here on the baby's behalf—on Sonia Marie's behalf. Regardless of whether or not we're dealing with an old will or a new one, Mr. Anderson and I are here to make sure that my granddaughter's interests are protected."

Leaving Harlan standing, she strode into the room, settled her designer-clad self into one of the game room chairs, crossed her long high-heeled legs, and then gave Les a cool appraisal. "Shall we get started then?" she asked.

Ali knew at once that Monique was one tough cookie. Short of someone bodily throwing her out of the room, she and her attorney weren't leaving.

Les looked questioningly at Ali. "By all means," Ali said. "Let's get on with it."

Les Jordan sighed. First he went around the room, making all the necessary introductions, saving Ali for last.

"I know who she is," Monique said shortly. "I've seen her before. On TV. Now tell us about the will."

"The truth is, a new will was prepared," Jordan continued. "It's been drawn up, but it was never signed. We expected to finalize this after the divorce hearing yesterday. Obviously that didn't happen, so the most recent last will and testament, the one that's still in effect, is the one that was drawn up eight years ago shortly after Paul's marriage to Ms. Reynolds here."

A file folder had been lying on the table in front of him. He opened it now and began to read. Ali only half listened. She was familiar with the provisions. Shortly after the wedding, she and Paul had signed similar documents. Ali had left behind a trust for Chris. Paul had named some charitable bequests. Other than those, they had left everything to each other. Ali remembered that they had signed the wills in some other attorney's office. At the time, it had seemed that Paul was going out of his way to protect Ali's interests. Now, though, under these changed circumstances, being Paul's sole beneficiary opened several cans of worms, not the least of which, Ali realized, would be Monique Ragsdale.

As Les Jordan read through the provisions—the charitable bequests as well as the personal ones—Monique became more and more agitated. The bottom line was clear. Ali Reynolds was still Paul Grayson's wife, and since much of what they owned was community property, it went to Ali.

"You mean to tell me that April and her baby get nothing?" Monique demanded. "How can that be? You drew up the new will. Why wasn't it signed?"

Les Jordan was exceedingly patient. "Paul and I had an appointment to sign the will yesterday afternoon after the divorce was final. He wanted to do it that way. Thought it would be cleaner somehow. We were scheduled to meet here at the house so he and April could both sign new documents."

"I knew Paul Grayson," Monique declared. "He was an honorable man. I can't believe he meant to leave either his intended bride or his child unprovided for."

Honorable? Ali thought to herself. With Paul Grayson's legal widow sitting right there in the room and with his pregnant not-bride sitting somewhere upstairs, that seemed an odd thing to say. You could call Paul any number of things, but honorable certainly wasn't one of them.

"Intended and legally married are two different things," Jordan pointed out.

"But still," Monique continued. "The only thing that

prevented him from marrying April was his tragic and untimely death. In fact, I happen to believe that's the whole reason he's dead. That whoever killed him did so just to make sure the marriage between my daughter and Paul Grayson never happened." The pointed look she cast in Ali's direction at the end of that little speech spoke volumes.

Ali's cheeks flushed. It was galling to have to sit in the room and have your husband's mistress's mother come right out and accuse you of murder. Ali was about to open her mouth to defend herself when Victor touched her arm. With a slight warning shake of his head he admonished her to keep quiet.

"We're all dealing with a good deal of emotional upheaval at the moment, Ms. Ragsdale," he said soothingly. "For right now, though, I think it would be best if we all refrained from tossing around unfounded allegations."

Les Jordan nodded in agreement. "Mr. Angeleri is right," he said. "We need to keep from being drawn into making any kind of accusations. As for the baby, there are laws on the books in the state of California that are specifically designed to deal with cases like this—laws that protect the interests of in utero or omitted off-spring. No doubt some funds would be made available from the estate to support the child and monies held in trust until he or she—"

"She," Monique supplied.

Jordan nodded. "Until she reaches her majority. Most likely a guardian *ad litem* would be appointed to protect the child's interests in the meantime."

"That's fine and good for the baby," Monique Ragsdale objected. "But what about my daughter? What happens to her? Does that mean she could be evicted and put out on the street?"

"No one here is suggesting any such thing, certainly not at this time," Les Jordan said. "But the truth is, as I told you earlier, your daughter is merely an intended wife as opposed to a wife in fact. Unless Mr. Grayson has made some kind of specific provisions for her, through the purchase of life insurance or something of that nature, I don't know of any legal remedies that would come into play that would allow your daughter to go against the will. That's not to say there aren't any, but none come readily to mind."

"What if you went ahead and finalized the divorce?" Monique's question was addressed to Ted Grantham.

"Excuse me?" he asked.

Monique was undaunted. "Harlan here has found a similar case in New Jersey where the divorce was finalized after the husband's death. That cleared the way for the property agreement to stand in court and made for simplified estate planning. The divorce also automatically negated the old will. In this case, that might work to Sonia's benefit."

"But not to mine," Ali said sharply.

"This isn't about you," Monique said firmly. "It's all about the baby."

"And what about me?" April asked. "Divorce or no, it sounds like I'm left with nothing."

Until April spoke, no one else gathered in the room had noticed her unannounced arrival. How long she had been outside the library door listening was anyone's guess. She clearly had changed her mind about going upstairs to dress since she stood in the doorway still wearing her nightgown and robe.

Monique leaped to her feet and hurried to her daughter. "You shouldn't be here," Monique said. "You should be upstairs resting."

"I don't need to rest," April protested. "I deserve to be part of this discussion. After all, it's my life, too. I need to know what's going on instead of the bunch of you talking about it behind my back. Besides, I already heard what he said. According to Paul's will everything goes to her." She nodded in Ali's direction. "It's so not fair. How can this be happening? It's like a nightmare or something. And where are all my friends? Who sent them away?"

"I did," Monique said. "And I'm sure others have called, but I sent them all to the answering service. And I posted a 'Do Not Disturb' sign out at the front door. I didn't want people bothering you at a time like this. And having too many people running around would just get in the way of the filming."

"But I *need* my friends," April returned. "I *need* the company more than I need the rest. You had no right to send my friends away."

All of which answered one of Ali's earlier questions as to the whereabouts of April's friends. And Ali noticed something else. Out on the terrace April had been grieving, but she had been a grieving grown-up. Now, with her mother in the room, April seemed to have reverted to some childhood script. She sounded even younger than she was—more like a petulant, demanding teenager than an adult.

Ignoring her mother's advice, April made her way

into the crowded room, where she sank into one of the swivel chairs. Pulling the gaping robe more tightly around her, she stared at Ali. "You were nice to me before," she said flatly, "but I guess this means things have changed. When do I have to leave, before the baby's born or after?"

"No one has said a word about your having to leave," Ali said. "And certainly not right now. With a baby due in a matter of days, you need to stay where you are until the lawyers can help us get things sorted out."

"How long does sorting-out take?" April asked. "And what's there to sort?"

Since Les Jordan had been effectively chairing the meeting, Ali looked at him for guidance.

He shrugged. "Uncomplicated estates can be settled in a matter of months," he said. "Complicated ones can take much longer than that, especially if other matters arise—like needing to liquidate property, for example. And there are always other legal issues that can cause indefinite delays."

He didn't spell out exactly what kind of "legal issues" he meant, but Ali had a pretty clear idea he was thinking about criminal proceedings. She guessed that everyone else in the room, with the possible exception of April herself, was making a similar assumption. Ali might be Paul's widow and the major beneficiary of his will, but she also knew that she wouldn't be allowed to inherit a dime as long as she was considered a suspect in his death. Until she was cleared, settling the estate would be stuck in neutral—and accumulating legal fees like crazy.

"What about the funeral?" April asked.

"What about it?"

"I'm twenty-five years old," April said. "I don't know anything about planning funerals." *I didn't either*, Ali thought, *but I figured it out*.

"You don't need to worry about any of that," Monique told her daughter. "I'll handle it all."

"No, you won't," April said. Her reply was forceful enough that it took everyone by surprise, most especially her mother. "Since I wasn't Paul's wife and since I'm not his widow, it isn't my place to handle it. And it isn't yours, either."

April looked at Ali as she spoke. Monique, on the other hand, seemed utterly astonished by this small but dry-eyed and very determined rebellion. Monique was so surprised, in fact, that Ali wondered if there had ever been another instance in which April had drawn a line in the sand and told her mother no in such unequivocal terms. Before Monique had a chance to say anything more, Ali stepped into the breach.

"My first husband died of cancer when I was about your age," she told April. "My son was born two months after his father died, so I do know a little of what you're going through. Planning Dean's funeral was hard work, but I needed to do it. And you'll need to do it, too. Funerals are really for the living, but they're also a major part of the grieving process. I'll be glad to help you plan it, if you want me to."

"Wait a minute," Monique objected. "April is my daughter. You can't just come horning in like this—"

"Mother," April said. "Stop." And then, to Ali she added, "Yes, I'd like you to help me. How long does planning a funeral take?"

"Not that long. Other than choosing a casket or an

urn and deciding on cremation or not, you really can't do much until after the coroner releases the body. In the case of a homicide, that could take several days. Only after the body is released can you establish a time for the services, arrange for flowers, get the announcements into the paper, and all of that."

"I've never even been to a funeral," April said. "Where do people hold them? At a church somewhere? Here at the house?"

"Not at the house," Ali said quickly. "And Paul wasn't someone I'd call a churchgoing kind of guy. So maybe the funeral home would be best for the service itself with a catered reception here at the house afterward."

"Do you send out invitations or something?" April asked.

She really is young, Ali thought.

"No, someone writes an obituary with an announcement at the end telling the time and place of the services and whether or not they're open to the public. That goes into the *Times.* Then whoever wants to come shows up."

April nodded. "You said funeral home. Which one?"

Ali remembered the form she had signed, the one the clerk in the coroner's office had handed her.

"When I went to Indio to do the identification, I signed a form in the Riverside County Coroner's Office. Once they're done with the body, it authorizes them to release it to the Three Palms Mortuary here in Beverly Hills," Ali answered. "I chose them because, years ago, they handled the services for Paul's mother. They did a good job. The facility is lovely, the chapel is spacious, and I remember the people were nice to deal with. And the funeral chapel is relatively close—only a mile or so away, on Sunset. But if you'd rather use someone else . . ."

"No," April said. "I'm sure they'll be fine."

"Wait a minute, April," Monique interjected. "This is ridiculous. You can't just let her walk in and take over everything. For God's sake, stand up for yourself, April. Take charge!"

"I am standing up for myself," April returned. "I'm going to do this my way, and Ali is going to help." She looked around at the faces of the legal eagles gathered there. "Is there anything else?"

Les Jordan shook his head. "Not that I know of," he said. "Not at this time."

"Good. I'm going back upstairs," April said. "And now I really am going to get dressed. I want to go out and check on the sudoku shoot."

The arms on the game chair were low. With April's bulging belly throwing her center of gravity off-kilter, it was a struggle for her to rise to her feet. Victor stood and gave her a hand up. Ali expected Monique to get up and follow her daughter out of the room, but she didn't. She stayed right where she was.

"April is my daughter," she said. "I'm not going to stand by and let you walk all over her and control the purse strings."

"No one is walking all over her," Les Jordan pointed out. "We're simply apprising her of the legal ramifications of her situation."

But Ali understood at once that Monique wasn't addressing the attorneys. She was talking to Ali directly, telling her to back off.

"Are we done here?" Victor asked.

"As far as I know," Les said.

"Good. We'll be going then. Come on, Ali. Helga."

Ali rose to her feet, aware of Monique's glare fastened on her. She walked past Monique toward the doorway, then turned and came back. "Your daughter's going through a terrible time right now," Ali said. "I have no intention of walking all over her. I'm trying to help."

"She doesn't need your help," Monique insisted. "Why would she? She has me."

Exactly, Ali thought as she followed Victor and Helga out the door. *Poor baby. Why would April need anyone else?*

{ CHAPTER 7 }

When Victor, Ali, and Helga emerged from the house, they discovered that Victor's Lincoln was blocked by a second huge RV, this one with the logo SUMO SUDOKU DRAGONSLAYER TEAM. In the process of shoehorning the second RV into the circular drive, the driver had taken out one of the gateposts and one side of the RV as well. Jesus, the gardener, and the guy who was apparently the driver were involved in a heated conversation about the incident with the entire discussion taking place in high-volume Spanish.

As the newly reinstalled mistress of Robert Lane, Ali supposed she should take a hand in the discussion, but since Jesus appeared to have the situation under control, she didn't. Ali had concerns that were far more compelling than fixing a broken gate.

She and Helga got into the Lincoln, and Victor waited outside until the damaged RV had been moved out of the way. Off to one side of the house, in the yard outside the pool house, Ali caught a glimpse of people looking on as a film crew followed the action of a bare-chested man who bent over, reached down, picked up one of the sudoku rocks, and then lugged it off. So the Sumo Sudoku contest was under way.

"Have you ever heard of a postmortem divorce?" Ali asked.

"It'll never happen," Helga replied. "For one thing, we'd be stupid to sign off on it. Just losing the marital deduction would cost a fortune in estate taxes. Besides, April's smarter than that—smarter than I gave her credit for, anyway."

"What do you mean?"

"I mean she looked around that room full of lawyers, figured out you were the softest touch in the place, and snuggled right up to you, driving her mother crazy in the process."

"Aren't you being a little cynical?" Ali asked. "April's in a tough position. I happen to know from firsthand experience what she's going through about now."

"Don't fall for it," Helga insisted. "She's just buttering you up because she figures you're the one who'll be doling out the money for her baby."

"What's wrong with that?" Ali asked. "Wasn't Ted Grantham trying to do the same thing—buttering me up—in order to be sure that his bill gets paid?"

"That's different," Helga returned. "April has a way better hand than Ted Grantham does. He isn't eight and a half months pregnant, and she is. Believe me, April is going to use that as a club. She'll play on your sympathy for all she's worth. She's got you pegged as being too nice to throw her out in the cold. Besides, she won the first round fair and square."

"What first round?" Ali asked.

"When you said you'd let her stay on in the house until after the baby is born. When it comes time for her to actually leave, I predict you'll have to evict her. And I agree with Ted, by the way. While settling the estate is in limbo, you need to request an inventory and appraisal of everything in the house. I've known plenty of women like April Gaddis in my time. She'll figure out what's worth stealing and what isn't and she'll make off with anything that isn't nailed down. And requiring a paternity test wouldn't be out of line, either."

It was ironic for Ali to find herself in the position of having to defend her dead husband's pregnant girlfriend to Helga Myerhoff, Ali's own divorce attorney. She was relieved and glad to change the subject when Victor opened the door and clambered into his seat.

He looked over at Ali and shook his head in seeming disgust. "What part of 'whatever you say may be held against you' don't you understand?"

"Excuse me?" Ali asked.

"Your blog," Victor said. "My assistant just called. She's been reading your blog on the Web—reading all about it, as they say. You have to understand it's not just what you say to the cops that can be held against you, Ali. It's what you say anywhere to anyone. Fang? You really called Paul Grayson Fang?"

"He's been Fang in my blog for a long time," Ali protested. "Since long before somebody killed him."

"Believe me, Detectives Sims and Taylor are going to love that. For right now, you're to say nothing more in your blog about this case, understood? For as long as this is an active investigation, commentary from you is off the table."

"Yes," Ali said. She felt stupid and chagrined. "And about Sims and Taylor . . ."

"What about them?" Victor asked sharply.

"They've evidently been in touch with April," Ali said. "She told me about it earlier, when we were out on the terrace."

"What did she say?"

"That they think Paul's killer escaped by leaving the car on the railroad tracks and then walking down the ties far enough so he was able to exit the tracks without being detected. They're speculating that he met up with an accomplice somewhere in the vicinity and they took off from there," Ali said.

Victor expelled a long sigh. "Which explains why they didn't find any footprints at the scene."

Ali nodded. "Yes," she said.

"That would also mean that the killer or killers were still in the general area at the time Paul died. Which, according to the receipts from the gas station and the restaurant in Blythe, would have placed you in the area as well."

Ali nodded again. She liked the way Victor immediately connected the dots even if she didn't like the dots he was connecting. "Yes," she said.

"My guess is, they're already going after your phone records then," Victor mused. "Trying to see who all you've contacted recently, to see if they can get a handle on who you might have enlisted as an accomplice."

"My phone records?" Ali demanded. "Isn't that illegal?"

"It's illegal to listen in on your phone calls without a warrant, but it's perfectly legal to look at your billing information to see who you called and who called you, as well as where you were and what cell phone towers were in use when those calls occurred."

"They can look at my phone records until they're blue in the face," Ali said. "They're not going to find anything. They're going to have to look elsewhere."

"If they look elsewhere," Victor responded.

"What do you mean, if?"

"Sims and Taylor have a high-profile case on their hands, one their bosses are going to want cleared in a hell of a hurry. They also have a likely suspect—you. I think there's a good chance that they'll work like crazy to make whatever evidence they have fit what they think happened, rather than looking very hard for what else might have happened or who else might have been involved."

"What other suspects are there?" Ali asked.

"You tell me," Victor returned. "April would have to be dumb as a stump to knock Paul Grayson off without knowing in advance that she was going to inherit."

"What about April's mother?" Ali asked.

"Ms. Ragsdale may bear looking into," Victor conceded.

"I think so, too," Helga agreed. "That woman is a piece of work. The very idea of our agreeing to a post-mortem divorce is ridiculous."

A few minutes later, Victor dropped Ali off at her hotel. A glance at her watch told her that, depending on traffic, her mother would probably be arriving within the next hour or so. She went upstairs to await Edie's arrival. While Ali waited, she logged on and found her in-box once again brimming with messages. Before she read any of them, however, she wrote a post of her own.

CUTLOOSEBLOG.COM
Saturday, September 17, 2005

Ali's first instinct was to begin her post with the words "On the advice of my attorney . . ." but then she remembered what Victor had said: "Anything you say can and will be held against you." So she went for something much less descriptive and also, to her way of thinking, much less real.

For the time being commentary from Babe
will be suspended due to my involvement in a
complex personal matter. As time allows, I will
continue to post appropriate or interesting
comments from readers. In the meantime, thank
you for your loyalty and your interest.
    Posted 11:12 A.M., September 17, 2005 by Babe

When she began reading through the e-mails, most of them had to do with the posting from Phyllis in Knoxville. Some correspondents seemed to agree that Phyllis had the right idea.

> *Dear Babe,*
> *Phyllis is right. Be nice to Twink and be nice to yourself. As ye sow so shall ye reap.*
>
> ANNA

> *Dear Babe,*
> *You suffered a terrible loss, too. More than one. Please know that you're in my thoughts and prayers.*
>
> LESLIE IN IOWA

Surprised by the number of people offering their condolences, Ali replied to all of them without necessarily posting them. Not all of the notes were kind, however.

> *Oh, great. Another Southern California celebrity murder by another "abused" media wife. The gossip columnists will go nuts. No doubt you'll hire yourself some high-priced attorney and get off scot-free. You people all make me sick. I hope you rot in hell.*

That one wasn't signed and didn't merit a response.

Dear Babe,
When I read the part about the homicide
detectives interviewing you, I couldn't believe
it, but then the cops always suspect the spouse,
although usually the killer is the husband instead
of the wife. Does that mean they think you did
it? Are they going to arrest you or are you just
a person of interest? If they do arrest you, my
nephew, Richard Dahlgood, is an attorney in L.A.
I don't know what he charges, but if you want to
get in touch with him, let me know and I'll give
you his numbers.

VELMA T IN LAGUNA

Ali wanted to tell Velma that she had all the legal
assistance she could handle about then. She had no
doubt that Velma's nephew was probably far more afford-
able than the hulking Victor Angeleri. But she was paying
the man too much to disregard his advice. She replied to
Velma with a carefully noncommittal thank-you.

Dear Velma,
Thank you for your concern. Please don't worry
about me. I have the situation well in hand.

BABE

The next e-mail stunned her.

Dear Ms. Reynolds,
Please forgive me for contacting you through

*your blog. I tried calling your home number in
Arizona. I left a message there, but it seems likely
you're here in California at the moment. My
name is Sheila Rosenburg. I'm a local (L.A.-area)
producer for Court TV. We would like to be in
touch with you whenever it might be convenient
for you regarding a possible interview. My contact
information is listed below.*

SHEILA ROSENBURG

The very idea that Paul's death had now become
fodder for the "true crime" network was nothing short
of chilling. If Court TV was on the job, could Fox's
Greta Van Susteren be far behind? And in that fanati-
cal crowd, Ali knew producers and commentators could
make as much of a story about what wasn't said as they
did about what was.

Dear Ms. Rosenburg,
*Thank you for your interest. I'm not granting any
interviews at this time. Should that change, I'll let
you know.*

REGARDS,
ALI REYNOLDS

The next one was a stunner.

Hey, Ali,
*How's it going. Long time no see. I have a line
on a possible job offer for you that'll put you back*

*where you belong—on live TV. If you're going to
be in L.A. anytime soon, let me know and I'll see
what I can do to set up an interview.*

JACKY

Jacky was short for Jack Jackson, Ali's agent—at
least he had been her agent. The words that came to
mind now were: more nerve than a bad tooth. In actual
fact, Jacky had been Ali's agent for a long time—from
her first on-air job out of college in Milwaukee to her
move from Fox News in New York to the L.A. anchor
desk. Ali had gotten the L.A. job on her own and without any help from Jacky, but he had been glad to take
his cut of the action. Then. But once she'd been let
go—once she'd been booted off the air and once she'd
made it clear that she wasn't going to take her age-based
firing lying down—Jacky had disappeared off the face
of the planet. He had stopped taking Ali's calls, hadn't
returned her e-mails, either.

She had understood what was going on well enough.
In television circles, network executives counted for
something. Paul Grayson had been the four-hundred-
pound gorilla, and no one had wanted to piss him off.
No doubt Jacky had read about what was going on and
had decided to distance himself, leaving Ali and her sty-
mied career to her own devices. Now, with Paul gone,
Jacky must have reached the sudden conclusion that Ali
Reynolds was bankable again. No doubt he expected to
be welcomed back with open arms. And his assumption
that she'd want to have him back rankled worse than
anything.

Screw you, Ali thought. *No vultures allowed.* With that she deleted Jacky's message.

The phone rang a few seconds later—the room phone. "There's someone down in the lobby who would like to see you, Ms. Reynolds," the smooth voice of the concierge said. "She says she's your mother. Would you like me to send her up?"

"Yes," Ali said. "Please do."

Ali stood in the open doorway of her room to greet Edie Larson when she arrived a few minutes later, dragging an immense roll-aboard bag behind her.

"I hope it's okay if I bunk with you," Edie said uncertainly.

"It's fine," Ali said, gesturing toward the king-sized bed.

"Did you know Dave Holman was coming?" Edie asked. "I ran into him down in the lobby. He was going to rent a room here, but then he found out how much they cost and almost had a heart attack, so he's gone to find someplace else to stay." Edie stopped in the middle of the room and turned around, slowly examining the plush surroundings. "Are you sure you can afford this?"

"Yes," Ali said, thinking back to her lawyer-filled morning and the news that over time she was bound to inherit a good deal of Paul Grayson's considerable fortune. In fact, she could afford to stay here now far more easily than she could have before. She closed the hallway door and turned to face her mother.

"So how are things?" Edie Larson asked. "And how are you?"

For some reason, those two questions, coming

from Edie, were enough to cause Ali's emotional dam to break. All the tears she hadn't shed in the coroner's office—all the tears she had put on hold and hadn't shed during her visit to the house on Robert Lane—burst through now. Sobbing, she let herself be pulled into her mother's arms—held and comforted—while Edie patted her shoulder and crooned soothing words.

"Shush now," Edie murmured. "It's going to be all right. You'll see. Now then, have you had any lunch?"

This was so typically Edie Larson that Ali had to smile through her tears. Edie's daughter might be a crazed killer on her way to the slammer, but Edie would move heaven and earth to be sure Ali was properly fed beforehand.

"Not yet," Ali said.

Edie heaved her oversized suitcase up onto the bed and unzipped it. "Now then," she said. "Let me hang up my clothes and put things away. I'll be able to think better once I get organized."

"When you finish, maybe we can go downstairs and have something to eat."

"Bad idea," Edie said. "We'd probably be better off ordering from room service."

"How come?" Ali asked.

"Because there are a lot of people milling around down in the lobby who looked like news people to me. I asked one of the helper guys, a doorman, I think, what they were doing. He said they were looking for you."

"For me?" echoed Ali.

"Not by name," Edie answered. "He said they were here because there's a 'murder suspect' reportedly stay-ing at the hotel right now. He said they're trying to get a glimpse of her. This may be California," Edie added, "but I'm assuming that even in L.A. there's not more than one murder suspect at a time staying in a place like this."

When Ali had worked the news desk, one of the rules had been that suspects weren't mentioned by name until they'd actually been charged with a crime. But that wouldn't help her. Her face had already turned up on camera the night before as she and Victor were leaving the coroner's office. And people had noticed. People had recognized her. She didn't know how they had managed to trace her to the hotel. Most likely someone had followed Victor's Lincoln when they left Robert Lane. Now, knowing they were here, Ali felt besieged.

"Room service sounds good to me," she said.

Half an hour later, Ali's cell phone rang. "How do people stand this traffic day in and day out?" Dave Holman wanted to know. "And it's not just during rush hour, either. It lasts all day long."

"Where are you?" Ali asked.

"Motel 6. That's a little more my speed than the place you're staying."

"Where?"

"Highway 101 and some other freeway, I-210, I think. The good thing is, I should be able to make my way back there from here on surface streets. The people driving on the freeways are nuts."

Ali had come to L.A. from New York. The metro area had seemed different to her but not entirely alien. Dave hailed from Sedona. She could see how foreign the city must seem to someone accustomed to living in small-town Arizona.

"Our room number is 703," she told him. "When you get back here to the hotel, come directly up to the room. Whatever you do, don't ask for me by name. Mom says there are reporters down in the lobby. One of them might be listening."

"No kidding," Dave returned. "I may be a hick, but when I met up with Edie a while ago down in the lobby, I did notice one or two reporters had been added to the mix."

"So we'll have lunch up here," Ali said. "From room service. What do you want?"

"A burger. Medium rare. No tofu!"

Ali laughed at that. "No tofu it is."

She called room service and ordered a burger for Dave and tortilla soup for Edie and herself. When she put down the phone, she found Edie studying her daughter's reflection in the mirror.

"Have you met her?" Edie asked.

"Met who?"

"April Gaddis," Edie replied. "Paul's fiancée."

"How do you know her name?" Ali asked.

Edie reached into a capacious purse and pulled out a handful of newspapers. "I stopped for coffee at that truck stop on the far side of Palm Springs and picked up a couple of newspapers," she replied. "I wanted to know what we were up against before I got here."

Edie laid the papers on the desk and then pulled out a brand-new spiral notebook. She opened the notebook to the first page, which was blank. "When Dave Holman is working a homicide, I know he always keeps a casebook," Edie added, picking up a pen. "I think we should do the same thing. I'm going to write down everything so we don't forget details. So tell me. What's April like?"

Under any other circumstance, Ali might have found her mother's businesslike approach amusing, but this wasn't funny. As Edie sat with her pen poised over paper, it was clear she wanted answers.

"Very young, very pretty, very pregnant," Ali said finally.

"And she was supposed to get married today," Edie said.

Ali nodded.

"Is she considered a suspect in Paul's murder?" Edie wanted to know.

"Probably not," Ali said. "No motive. Had the divorce been finalized and the wedding ceremony performed, it might be a different story, but when the will was read this morning, I was still Paul's legal wife and primary beneficiary. If April was going to knock him off, surely she would have been smart enough to wait until they were actually married."

"Is she that smart?" Edie asked.

Ali thought about what Helga had said—about April being smart enough to throw herself on Ali's mercy. "I think so," Ali responded.

"Who else would have a motive then?" Edie asked. She was approaching the problem in her accustomed manner—with no nonsense and plenty of common sense. "Is there a chance there's another man in the picture?" she added. "If money isn't the motivating factor, maybe something else is—like jealousy, for example. From what I see on TV, jealousy works."

Ali had thought about April Gaddis and Paul Grayson primarily in terms of the two of them cheating on her. The idea that they might have been cheating on each other had never crossed her mind.

"It's possible, I suppose," Ali said dubiously. She wasn't entirely convinced.

"Of course it is," Edie declared. "If Paul would cheat on you, he'd cheat on her, too. That's what your father says: Once a cheat, always a cheat. So the first thing we have to do is find out everything there is to know about April Gaddis."

"We should ask Christopher about that," Ali said. "He knew about April long before I did. She's related to some friend of his. April was working for Paul as his administrative assistant, but I don't know which came first, the chicken or the egg—the job or the affair. I think it's likely that he got her the job so she could earn enough money to support herself. That way there wouldn't be a paper trail linking money from him to her."

"Right, a little prenuptial nepotism never hurt anybody," Edie observed. "So I'll ask Christopher about April."

"I met her mother," Ali supplied.

"April's mother?" Edie asked. "You have?"

"Her name's Monique Ragsdale. She came to the house this morning to meet with the attorneys. She claims she's looking out for the interests of the baby. I suspect she's mostly looking out for herself. She came hoping we'd agree to a postmortem divorce decree."

"You can't divorce someone after they're dead, can you?"

"Helga doesn't think so," Ali said.

There was a knock on the door. When Ali opened

it, the room service trolley was waiting out in the hallway, and so was Dave Holman. His broad-shouldered, military bearing was something Ali really needed about then—something she welcomed. Reaching past the waiter, she gave Dave a brief but heartfelt hug.

"Thanks for coming," she said.

"Wouldn't have missed it," he said.

While the waiter set up a table out on the deck, Dave prowled the room. "This one's a little nicer than mine," he said. "There's no room service at Motel 6, but there's a Denny's up the block, so I'll live." He peered over Edie's shoulder at the notebook.

"Just trying to get an idea of who all's involved," she explained.

"Good work," he said.

All through lunch, Edie and Dave continued to pepper Ali with questions while Edie took copious notes. Once again Ali recalled what Victor had told her: "Anything you say . . ." But surely what she told her own mother and her good friend Dave couldn't hurt her, could it? Especially since everything she said was the truth.

They were just finishing lunch when the phone rang. "Ted Grantham here," he said. "This is a bit awkward, but . . ."

"What is it?"

"April called while Les and I were having lunch," he said. "I didn't get the message until I came back to the office. She said she was having a problem with her mother about planning the funeral. She wanted to talk to you about it if you wouldn't mind coming back up to the house to see her."

"Of course," Ali said. "I'll be glad to."

"Glad to what?" Edie asked when Ali got off the phone.

"April wants me to come back up to the house and talk about funeral arrangements."

"With you?" Dave demanded.

"Yes. With me." Ali was already searching the room for her purse and her keys.

"How come?" Dave wanted to know.

"Because she's twenty-five years old and doesn't know how to go about handling all those details."

"Shouldn't her mother help her with that?" Dave asked.

"April doesn't want her mother involved."

"Wait a minute," Dave said. "Your dead ex-husband's girlfriend is arguing with her own mother about Paul Grayson's funeral arrangements, and she expects you to walk right into the middle of it? What's wrong with this picture?"

"You don't understand," Ali said. "You haven't met Monique Ragsdale. I have."

"I do understand," Dave said. "All too well. Stay out of it, Ali. Run, do not walk, in the opposite direction."

Ali looked at Dave. He was a nice enough man, but he had no idea what it was like to be pregnant with someone's baby and to have that person snatched out of your life. No matter who April Gaddis was or whose baby she was carrying, at this point it was impossible for Ali to feel anything but compassion for her.

"April asked for my help. I'm going to give it to her," Ali said.

"Well then," Edie declared. "If you're going, so are we."

"All right," Dave said glumly. "But when it all goes to hell, just remember—I told you so."

Ali called down to the desk for her car. "This is Ali Reynolds," she added after relaying her valet parking ticket number to the bell captain. "Are there still reporters down there looking for me?"

"Yes," he replied. "I'm afraid there are."

"Is there a chance you could smuggle me out of the building without my being seen?"

"Sure. I could come up and get you in the service elevator and take you out the back way, through the kitchen."

"Would you?"

"Of course."

Dave shook his head the whole way down in the service elevator and raised a disapproving eyebrow at the size of the tip Ali handed over to the bellman, but the ploy worked. Ali was relieved that in the paparazzi bidding wars, her tip was large enough to allow them to exit the hotel without meeting up with even one of the waiting reporters.

With Edie in the backseat of the Cayenne, Ali drove back up the hill to Robert Lane. The broken front gate was still open, but filming had ended for the day. The Sumo Sudoku RVs were nowhere in evidence. The film crews had pulled up stakes and gone home, too. Leading the way to the front door, Ali was surprised to find it ajar. The DO NOT DISTURB sign had been removed. She paused long enough to ring the bell, but no one answered.

The entire entryway was awash in banks of floral bouquets, even more than had been there earlier.

"Hello?" Ali called. "April? Anybody home?"

There was no answer.

With Dave and Edie trailing behind, Ali ventured farther into the house. They found Monique Ragsdale lying sprawled at the bottom of the stairway. While Dave bent over the stricken woman and checked for a pulse, Ali dialed 911.

"Is she still breathing?" Ali demanded.

"Barely."

"Nine-one-one," the operator responded. "What are you reporting?"

"Someone's fallen," Ali found herself yelling into the phone. "She's fallen down a flight of stairs."

"Is she conscious?" the operator asked.

"No! She's barely breathing. Send someone. Hurry."

"Units are on the way," the operator said. "They'll be there soon."

Not soon enough, Ali thought. *Not nearly soon enough.*

"And your name is?"

"Ali," she answered. "Alison Reynolds."

"You just stay on the line with me, Ms. Reynolds. Help is on the way."

{ CHAPTER 8 }

Ali remained on the phone with the emergency operators while Dave stayed with Monique. Edie was dispatched to the upstairs bedrooms for a blanket to cover the injured woman. While she was at it, she searched through the rest of the house to see if anyone else was home.

"No one's here," she reported. "No one at all."

"Not even the cook?" Ali asked. "Did you check the kitchen?"

"I looked everywhere," Edie replied. "The whole house is empty."

The EMTs arrived within minutes. As they worked to shift Monique onto a board in order to load her onto a gurney, Ali spotted a cell phone and a key ring lying on the floor. She grabbed the phone, opened it, and hit the "redial" button. The words "April Cell" appeared on the screen.

"Where will you take her?" Ali asked one of the EMTs.

"The ER at Cedars-Sinai," he said.

Ali pressed the "talk" button and was disappointed when, instead of being answered, her call to April went straight to voice mail.

"April," Ali said urgently. "It's Ali Reynolds. Call me back as soon as you get this message. Your mother has fallen down the stairs. The EMTs are taking her to Cedars-Sinai. You may want to meet us there."

When she finished the call, Ali slipped the phone into her pocket.

"You shouldn't have touched that," Dave observed.

"Why not?" Ali asked. "I needed to get hold of April to let her know what's happened."

"If this turns out to be a crime scene, you've contaminated some of the evidence."

"A crime scene?" Ali repeated. "What crime scene? She fell."

"After she and her daughter quarreled," Dave pointed out. "You should put it back."

Ali looked around at the field of debris being left behind by the EMTs. The crime scene was contaminated, all right, and not just by her.

"I'm not putting it back," Ali insisted. "I told April to call me back on this number when she gets the message."

Dave shot her an exasperated look and then went to greet the pair of uniformed police officers who had arrived on the scene as the gurney was being wheeled out the front door.

Ali was still holding her car keys. She thrust them into her mother's hands. "I'm going to the hospital," Ali said. "Once Dave finishes with the cops, the two of you can come to the hospital in my car."

"But how do we get there?" Edie wanted to know.

"Don't worry," she said. "Use the GPS. You should be able to key Cedars-Sinai into it, and it'll lead you straight there."

"But—"

"No buts, Mom," Ali returned. "I'm going."

By the time she got outside, the doors on the ambulance had already slammed shut. Knowing she wouldn't be allowed to ride in that anyway, Ali went looking for an alternative. By then a fire department supervisor had arrived on the scene. After some persuading, Ali managed to convince the driver to take her along to the hospital.

"You're a relative?" he asked.

Mentally Ali thought through her actual connection to Monique Ragsdale: *"the mother of my murdered husband's pregnant girlfriend."*

That would sound more than slightly suspect. "Yes," Ali said. And let it go at that.

By the time Ali arrived at the entrance to the ER, Monique had already been wheeled inside and out of sight. Ali started toward the registration desk and then stopped. There was no point in even talking to those people. She knew nothing—no social security numbers, no insurance information. Saying she was a relative might have been enough to bum a ride to the hospital, but it wasn't going to wash with some sharp-eyed receptionist whose main purpose in life was to ascertain who would be responsible for authorizing lifesaving treatment and/or paying the bill.

Walking to one of the few unoccupied chairs in the room, Ali took Monique's phone out of her pocket and once again hit "redial." Still April didn't answer.

Where the hell are you? Ali wondered in frustration. *Why don't you answer?*

Gradually, the sights, sounds, and, even more, the smells of the waiting room assailed her. She had been pregnant the whole time Dean was sick. While he struggled with cancer, she had struggled with morning sickness, sitting in ER and hospital waiting rooms and clutching her own barf bucket. Being there brought all the memories back with awful clarity.

Around the room people sat huddled in their own private miseries. An older woman, in a wheelchair and on oxygen, sat with her eyes closed while the old man next to her periodically patted her hand. A few feet away from Ali, a feverish-looking toddler wailed inconsolably while his young mother, speaking in Spanish, tried in vain to comfort him. Then, with no warning, the anguished wail suddenly devolved into a spasm of projectile vomiting.

Ali knew that active puking or bleeding was the key to getting ER attention, and this was no exception. A nurse appeared from behind a curtained doorway, collected the sick baby and his mother, and then disappeared again. In less than a minute, a janitor, wearing gloves and a face mask, was there to clean up the mess. Meantime, a hugely pregnant young woman, also Hispanic, walked into the lobby on her own. At the receptionist desk, though, she was hit by a contraction that brought her to her knees. Someone grabbed a nearby wheelchair and whisked her away as well.

Living and dying, Ali thought. *Coming and going. That's what hospitals are all about.*

She tried April's number again, with the same result, then Ali closed her eyes and tried to shut all this out; tried to make it go away. But it didn't work. She was back in Chicago, lost in that awful time more than twenty years ago. Back in her own peculiar version of hell.

"Ms. Reynolds." A voice from far away pierced her reverie. "Ms. Alison Reynolds. Would you please come to the registration desk?"

As Ali rose to answer the summons, a phone rang. It wasn't her ring and so at first she didn't realize it was for her. Then Monique's phone began to vibrate as well as ring.

"Mom?" April asked.

"It's not your mother," Ali interjected. "It's me. Ali. Where are you? Did you get my messages?"

"I went for a drive. I had to get away for a while. The walls were closing in on me. I couldn't stand to be in the house a minute longer. But what are you doing on my mother's phone? I saw that she had called three times. I didn't bother listening to the messages. There's no point. She's always bossing me around and saying the same thing, over and over."

"The messages weren't from your mother," Ali said firmly. "They're from me, April, all of them. Your mother's been hurt. She's in the ER at Cedars-Sinai. You need to get here as soon as you can. Where are you?"

"Hurt? What do you mean, hurt?"

"She fell down the stairs at the house. She must have hit her head, either on the way down or on the tile floor at the bottom of the staircase."

There was a pause—a long pause. "Is it like, you know, bad?" April asked.

"I don't know how bad it is," Ali returned. "Since I'm not a blood relative, the people here at the hospital won't tell me anything."

By now Ali had reached the registration desk, where a woman seated in front of a computer terminal glared at Ali impatiently, waiting for her to finish the call.

"You brought Ms. Ragsdale in?" the receptionist asked. "We're going to need some information."

Ali thrust Monique's cell phone in the woman's direction. "There's no point in talking to me because I don't know anything. This is April Gaddis, Monique Ragsdale's daughter," she added. "You should probably talk to her."

The receptionist took the cell phone and handed it over to the same nurse who had come to collect the puking toddler. About that time two uniformed LAPD officers—a man and a woman—made their way into the ER. Ali recognized them at once. They were the same officers Ali had passed as she sprinted out of the house on Robert Lane intent on hitching a ride to the hospital. Unfortunately, three other people followed the two cops. Two of them carried cameras—one still and one video. The reporters were still on the hunt, and this trio had just gotten lucky.

The officers spotted Ali standing near the reception desk and hurried toward her. "Ms. Reynolds?" the female officer asked. "Could we speak to you for a moment, please?"

The flurry of activity that marked the arrival of the cops and the cameras caused every head in the waiting room to swivel curiously in Ali's direction. The room went totally silent as everyone strained to hear her answer.

"Yes, of course," she said. "How can I help?"

"I'm Officer Oliveras. We understand you're the person who found Ms. Ragsdale at the bottom of the stairs?" she asked.

"Yes," Ali answered. "That's correct."

"Can you tell us how you came to be there?" That question came from Officer Oliveras's partner, one Dale Ramsey.

"Monique's . . . that is, Ms. Ragsdale's daughter, April Gaddis, sent a message to me and asked me to come there—to the house. April said she needed my help."

"With what?" Ramsey asked.

"With making funeral arrangements," Ali began, then she paused and looked around the room. All ears seemed to be cocked in her direction. "It's all rather complicated," she added.

Officer Oliveras didn't smile. "Maybe you'd rather speak to us in a somewhat more private setting," she offered. "Our squad car is right outside."

The idea of being closeted in a vehicle with two more inquisitive cops didn't sound all that appealing, especially if there were photographers here ready to capture each and every vivid detail on film.

"No," Ali said quickly. "This is fine. I was sitting over there in the corner. Maybe we could do this there."

She led the cops into an area where the distinct odor of puke, barely covered by some astringent cleaning solution, still lingered in the air. Officer Oliveras followed Ali while Officer Ramsey rounded on the reporters.

"All right, you bozos," he said. "Enough! Get the hell out of here. Can't you see there are sick people here? You're botherin' 'em."

"So," Officer Oliveras said to Ali. "We're given to understand that the house where this happened, the house on Robert Lane, actually belongs to you?"

"Supposedly," Ali said. "But all that's pretty much in a state of confusion right now. You see, my husband died the night before last. Because our divorce hadn't been finalized and because his will hadn't been changed, the house evidently comes to me."

"And Ms. Ragsdale is the mother of your ex-husband's intended bride."

"Yes," Ali said. "That's correct."

"And you know her?"

"We've met," Ali admitted. "Only this morning. We were at a meeting together there at the house—a meeting with our several attorneys."

"Where you discussed this will situation—where your husband left everything to you and nothing to Ms. Ragsdale's daughter, the mother of your husband's baby?"

"Yes," Ali said, although her answer was barely audible. It was difficult to speak when what she was hearing loud and clear in her head were Victor Angeleri's words: "What part of 'whatever you say' don't you understand?"

"Should I have an attorney with me when I'm answering these questions?" Ali asked.

Officer Oliveras's face darkened. "It's up to you," she said. "If you feel you need one, that's fine, but at this point, all we're trying to do is get a handle on who all was there at the house this morning and why."

"We gathered there for a reading of my husband's will," Ali answered after a pause. "I was there along with April Gaddis, my husband's fiancée; Ms. Ragsdale; and then four attorneys. No, wait. There were five attorneys actually, counting Ms. Ragsdale's."

Ali reeled off each of the several attorneys' names while Officer Oliveras took notes.

"You say this last one, Mr. Anderson, is Ms. Ragsdale's attorney?" Oliveras asked. "Why would she need one? Is she a beneficiary under the will?"

It didn't seem wise to mention the possibility of a postmortem divorce. That wasn't necessarily lying. "No," Ali said finally. "Mr. Anderson was there ostensibly to protect the rights of the unborn baby. My understanding is, however, that regardless of whether or not the baby is named in the will, she'll still benefit from it."

"The baby?" Oliveras asked.

Ali nodded.

"You already know the baby's a girl then?"

"Yes."

Officer Ramsey sighed and shook his head impatiently, as though all the marital back-and-forthing was boring him to tears.

"If you and Ms. Ragsdale met just this morning, it's fair to assume you didn't have any particular bone of contention with her?"

"No. None at all."

"Was anyone else there?"

Ali did her best to recall everyone else—the cook; Jesus, the gardener; Tracy McLaughlin and the Sumo Sudoku people along with the accompanying film crew. Of those the only name she knew for sure was that of the interviewer, Sandy Quijada.

"All right now," Oliveras said. "Tell me again why was it you went back to the house this afternoon."

"April called and invited me over. Or rather, she called Ted Grantham's office and left a message asking me to come over and help her work on making funeral arrangements."

"For your ex-husband?"

"Yes."

"You must have a pretty cordial relationship with your husband's fiancée," Oliveras observed. "It seems to me she would have asked someone else for help with that kind of thing—her mother, for example."

This was exactly what Dave had said when he had warned Ali to stay away. And, as he had predicted, things were indeed going to hell.

At that moment April herself came charging through the ER's automatic doors. Her eyes were wide, her skin deathly pale. Panting, she raced up to the receptionist, who, after only a few murmured words of conversation, immediately summoned the nurse who was still holding Monique's cell phone. With no more formalities than that, April was handed the phone and then ushered through the curtains and back into the treatment rooms.

Across the crowded waiting room another baby started to cry. An ambulance arrived, sirens blaring, and discharged a new gurney adding a new set of stricken relatives into the mix. But Ali paid almost no attention to any of that. She knew without having to be told that Monique Ragsdale's condition had to be grave at best. The only thing that rushed anyone past loyal ER gatekeepers was the reality that someone in one of the back rooms was hanging by a thread between life and death.

"I guess," Ali said vaguely. "She was probably just feeling overwhelmed. That was April, by the way—the woman they just took back into the treatment rooms."

Officer Oliveras exhibited no interest in April, however. She was still focused on Ali, until there was yet another flurry of activity near the front door. To Ali's immense relief, Victor Angeleri barged into the room and stopped just inside the door. With a graceful pivot that belied his size, he took in the entire room at a glance and then strode toward the corner where Ali was huddled with the two cops.

"What's going on here?" Victor Angeleri demanded.

Once again the accidental audience in the ER subsided into a spellbound silence.

"How did you get here?" Ali wanted to know. "Who called you?"

"That's immaterial. The point is, what's going on with these officers? What kinds of questions are they asking you, and did they read you your rights?"

"You're Ms. Reynolds's attorney, I assume?" Officer Ramsey inquired. The two men were about the same height, but Victor outweighed the younger man by a good third.

"Yes, I'm her attorney," Victor declared forcefully. "And until I have a chance to confer with my client, this discussion is over."

Somewhere a flash went off. Ali had no doubt that every word of the conversation was being recorded for posterity—or, more likely, for the evening news.

Edie Larson and Dave Holman rushed through the ER doors and joined the mix. "Sorry it took us so long to get here," Edie said. "I just couldn't figure out how to make the GSP thingy work."

But seeing her mother's face answered at least one of Ali's questions. No doubt Edie Larson had been the one who called Victor Angeleri into the fray. Some other time, Ali might have reacted badly to this kind of parental interference. This time she was simply grateful.

April staggered through the curtains and reentered the waiting room. She seemed dazed and uncomprehending. Excusing herself, Ali hurried over to her. "Are you all right?"

"They're taking her to surgery," April managed. "The

doctor said she hit her head. Her brain's swelling. If they can't relieve the pressure, she may die."

With that, April buried her head in Ali's shoulder and began to weep. "How can this be happening on top of everything else?" she sobbed. "I can't believe it!"

"This would be Ms. Gaddis then?" Officer Ramsey asked, sidling over to them.

Ali simply looked at him. "Yes," she said, "but as you can see, this is not the time to speak to her. What do you want to do, April? Go to the surgical floor waiting room? Go home? What?"

"The surgery will take hours," April managed. "I think I need to go home."

"You can't go home," Officer Ramsey interjected. "It's a crime scene."

"Crime scene?" April repeated. "My home is a crime scene? What are you talking about?"

"One of our forensics teams is going over it right now. We think it's possible that what happened to your mother is actually a case of attempted homicide."

"But they told me she fell," April objected.

"She may have been pushed. Until we complete our investigation, that house is off-limits and no one goes there."

"What am I going to do then?" April wailed. "Where do I go?"

"Call your hotel, Ali," Victor ordered, taking charge. "See if they have a room available where she can stay." Then he rounded on Officer Ramsey. "As far as asking questions of Ms. Gaddis? Right now that's off the table. She's in no condition to be interviewed by anyone. She's pregnant, her fiancé has been murdered, and her mother is undergoing emergency surgery. If you ask her even one question, buddy-boy, I'll have you and your partner up on charges of police brutality so fast it'll make your head swim."

Officer Ramsey seemed ready to object, but Oliveras silenced him with a single but definitive shake of her head. "All right," she said. "We can talk to her later. Just call and let us know where she ends up."

The cops disappeared shortly thereafter. Their departure removed a lot of the drama from the room. With their attention lagging, the other occupants turned to their own, more pressing physical ailments and bodily concerns.

Ali and company made the return trip to their hotel room in much the same way they had exited hours before—through the back door and, with the help of the bell captain, up the service elevator. An hour later April was wrapped in a thick terry-cloth robe and tucked into a bed in the darkened bedroom of a two-room suite—the only room available on that floor—just down the hall from the one Ali was sharing with her mother. Once April was settled in, Ali went out into the living room, closing the bedroom door behind her.

"Is she asleep?" Victor asked.

"Resting," Ali said. "Not asleep. She asked the hospital to call my cell once her mother's in the recovery room. Then we'll take April back to the hospital."

Victor Angeleri was seated at the desk in the corner, staring morosely at the telephone. He nodded absently.

"You were talking to someone on the phone?" Ali asked.

He nodded again.

"Did you find out why those cops are so interested in talking to me?"

"Unfortunately, yes. Somebody's leaked the contents of Grayson's will to the press," Victor replied. "That means that now the whole world knows that despite your marital difficulties, you're still your husband's primary beneficiary. As far as John Q. Public is concerned, that makes you a prime suspect in Paul Grayson's murder. And the cops are going to be operating on that same wavelength. I expect we'll be hearing from Detectives Sims and Taylor again real soon."

"How can information about the will be out in public?" Ali demanded. "The will hasn't been filed in court, so it isn't a matter of public record. Who would have leaked it?"

"Good question. Presumably one of my erstwhile colleagues from this morning's meeting. I think I can make a fairly educated guess as to which one."

"But isn't that illegal?" Ali objected. "Doesn't it violate attorney-client privilege?"

"Of course it does," Victor returned. "And once I figure out who's responsible, you can bet I'll have his *cojones,* but for right now we have to live with the consequences of those revelations and with the fact that you're now a suspect in two incidents rather than just the one."

"Two?" Ali asked.

"One homicide and one attempted homicide."

"So now I'm supposedly responsible for what happened to Monique Ragsdale, too? How come? I barely know the woman."

"By showing up this morning armed with that cocka-
mamie postmortem divorce attorney, Monique Ragsdale
as good as declared war on you. That's certainly how it's
going to look—as though the two of you were in some
kind of a turf dispute. I can see exactly how it'll play out
in court, a David and Goliath routine. Monique will be
portrayed as a sympathetic character, selflessly trying
to protect the welfare of her daughter and her unborn
grandchild. You'll be depicted as the greedy ex-wife
defending her territory and her pocketbook by taking
the bothersome grandma out of the picture."

"But Monique fell down the stairs," Ali objected.
"That's not my fault."

"What if she was pushed?" Victor returned. "I know
how cops think. You're already on their radar as a suspect in Paul's death. They're going to operate on the
premise that if you're good for one homicide, you're
good for another."

"But I have an ironclad alibi," Ali objected. "I left the
house at the same time you did. You and Helga brought
me back here to the hotel. I was here in my room all afternoon, first with my mother and later with Dave Holman.
How could I possibly be responsible?"

Victor shrugged. "The cops have already decided
that at least two people were involved in what happened to your husband. If you had an accomplice in
that case, you'd be likely to have an accomplice for this
one as well."

"But I didn't *do* it," Ali insisted. "Mom, Dave, and
I went to the house together. That's when we found
her."

"Do you know how many people who 'discover' bodies end up being the doers?" Victor asked. "And tell me this. If you went to the house and no one was home, how did you get inside?"

"Through the front door. I rang the bell, but no one answered. Then, since the door was open, we went in."

"Didn't that strike you as unusual, that the door would be left open like that?"

"I didn't think about it at the time because I thought April was home. With the big crew involved in the shoot, there had been people coming and going all day long."

"Do you still have keys to the house?"

"Probably," Ali answered. "Back home in Sedona somewhere, but I certainly didn't bring them along, and I doubt they'd work anyway. I expect Paul would have changed the locks as soon as I moved out. I'm sure I would have."

"All right," Victor said. "Now tell me about the telephone."

"What telephone?" Ali asked.

"Come on. Don't play dumb. Monique's cell phone—the one you lifted from the crime scene. That's called evidence tampering. When the cops find out about it—if they find out about it—they're going to go nuts."

"The EMTs were busy hauling Monique off to the hospital when I noticed the phone was lying there on the floor," Ali explained. "By then I knew April wasn't home. I needed to reach her so I could let her know what was happening. I was sure her cell phone number would be in her mother's call records, and it was. How else was I supposed to find her number?"

"You could have called Ted Grantham back," Victor pointed out. "But you didn't. For right now the cops haven't noticed the phone issue. If they end up figuring out you took it, then we'll have to decide how to handle it. Now, what's the deal with Dave Holman?"

"What about him?"

"Are you an item or what?"

"Dave's good friends with my parents, and he's a friend of mine, too—a homicide detective for Yavapai County over in Arizona. But we aren't an 'item.'"

"What's he doing here then?"

"He drove over from Lake Havasu to help out."

"He should go home," Victor said simply. "So should your mother. I have my own team of investigators working on this case. What I don't need is a bunch of people—amateurs or otherwise—blundering around and muddying the waters. Having your mother and Dave here is going to be more of a hindrance than a help. Anything you say to them is going to be fair game for whatever detectives are doing follow-up on either one of these two cases. They'll ask Dave or your mother what you've said, and they'll end up being required to answer truthfully. So you can't confide in them—not at all. Understand?"

"It's too late," Ali said bleakly. "I already did."

And for the first time in all this, she actually felt afraid.

{ CHAPTER 9 }

Victor finally left. For a long time afterward, Ali sat alone in the living room area of April's suite mulling her situation. What if Monique Ragsdale didn't survive? Would Ali really be a suspect in her death as well? Could the cops turn Monique's mere threat of litigation into a motive for murder?

From what Ali had seen, Monique's fall had looked like an accident, but was it really? And speaking of accidents, what about the Sumo Sudoku boulder that had come flying in Ali's own direction? That, too, had appeared to be nothing more than an accident caused by an overloaded wheelbarrow, but what if it wasn't?

Pushing away that worrisome thought, Ali decided to track down how much of the story had surfaced in the media. Rather than switching on the television and possibly waking April, Ali did as she had so often done in the months since she had fled L.A., her former job, and her foundering marriage—she turned to her computer and to her blog and to the cyber support network from cutlooseblog.com that had sustained her through some pretty dark times.

Dear Ali, or I suppose I should say, Dear Babe,
When they booted you off the air months ago, I
always knew you'd be back on TV here in L.A.
eventually. I just didn't think it would be like this.
I saw what they showed on the news the other

*night when you were leaving the coroner's office
in Indio. That young woman they replaced you
with was so damned smug as she was reading the
story. I wanted to slap her. She didn't come right
out and mention you by name and say you were
a suspect in whatever had happened to your ex,
but people recognized you. I recognized you, even
though you weren't wearing makeup or anything.
And that big guy, Victor, was there with you.
Anybody who follows criminal cases in Southern California knows what he's all about. Why
would you need a big-time defense attorney if you
weren't a defendant?*

*All I'm trying to say is there are lots of us
out here who are still real fans of yours and who
think you're being sold down the river. Again. So
be strong. Know that people—people you don't
even know—are praying for you every day. I'm
one of them.*

CRYSTAL RYAN, SHERMAN OAKS,
CA

She didn't post Crystal's note, but wanting to say
something in reply—something that wouldn't get her
in trouble with Victor Angeleri—Ali penned a simple
response that said nothing yet covered all the bases.

*Dear Crystal,
Thank you for your support.*

ALI REYNOLDS

Dear Babe,
Have you called my nephew yet? From what
they're saying on the news, I think you'd better. It
sounds like things are getting more complicated
all the time.

VELMA T IN LAGUNA

Yes, Ali thought. *Things are getting more compli-*
cated. No, I haven't called your nephew, and I probably
won't.

She sent Velma the same note she had sent to Crystal. That was Ali's best bet for the moment—respond but do not engage. Keep a low profile.

Dear Ms. Reynolds,
After what happened to you, I can't believe you'd
do the same thing to my uncle. You should be
ashamed.

ANDREA MORALES

Ali studied that one for a very long time. She had no idea who Andrea Morales was, much less who the woman's uncle might be or what Ali could possibly have done to him. In the end, she felt she had to defend herself by sending a response.

Dear Andrea,
I'm sorry, but I'm unaware of who your uncle is or
what it is you believe I may have done to him. If
it's something for which I should offer an apology,

please let me know. I would appreciate it if you
could supply some additional information which
would allow me to be more knowledgeable about
this situation.

Thank you.

ALISON REYNOLDS

The next one was even more disturbing.

Hmmmm. Let me get this straight. Your soon-to-
be-ex-husband died unexpectedly without having
a chance to unload you by slipping loose from
that little gold tie that binds? Too bad somebody
didn't warn the poor guy about black widows.
I think he was married to one. RIP, Fang. You
deserved better. As for you, "Babe"? I hope you get
what you deserve.

LANCE-A-LOT

Black widow, Ali thought. *Thanks-a-lot. Let's hope*
this one doesn't hit the blogosphere. If it does, it'll go like
wildfire.

She didn't reply to that one.

Ali's cell phone rang just then. She hurried to answer
it, thinking it would be the hospital. It wasn't.

"Aunt Ali?"

She recognized the voice of ten-year-old Matt Bernard. Months earlier, Matt's mother, Ali's childhood
friend Reenie Bernard, had been murdered. In the
messy aftermath of Reenie's death, her husband, a pro-

fessor at Northern Arizona University, had taken off on sabbatical with a new wife in tow and had left his two children, Matt and his younger sister, Julie, in the care of their maternal grandparents in Cottonwood. Ali had stayed in touch with Reenie's two kids as much as possible. Thanks to their grandfather's pet allergies, Ali was also looking after their cat, the plug-ugly, one-eared, sixteen-pound wonder, Samantha.

"Hi, Matt."

"How's Sam?"

"Sam's fine," Ali said. She didn't know that with absolute certainty, but she felt confident in saying so.

"Grandpa and Grandma are driving to Sedona tomorrow afternoon after church," Matt went on. "I was wondering if Julie and I could come by your house for a while to visit and play with Sam."

That was the weird thing about cell phones. Callers dial numbers with a complete mental image of where the other person is and what he or she is doing. No doubt Matt was envisioning Ali in her spacious mobile home in Sedona, curled up on her living room sofa with Sam right there beside her. Instead, Ali was several hundred miles away, sitting in a hotel room, and embroiled in a set of circumstances that might well keep her from returning to Sedona for some time. Ali didn't want to go into any of those messy details with Matthew Bernard right then. Or ever.

"Oh, Matt," she said. "I'm so sorry. I've been called out of town. I won't be there tomorrow."

"Who's taking care of Sam then?" he asked.

"My dad," Ali said. "He loves cats, and they love him. If you're coming up in the afternoon, after the

Sugar Loaf is closed for the day, maybe you could visit with Sam at my parents' house."

Matt sounded dubious. "Wouldn't your father mind?"

Ali thought about Bob Larson, a man who adored animals and little kids. "As long as it's after hours, I'm sure he'd be thrilled to have you, but why don't you call him and ask?"

"I think that would be weird." Suddenly Matt seemed stricken with an uncharacteristic case of shyness. "I mean, I don't really know him."

"By the time you and Julie spend Sunday afternoon with him, you will know him," Ali countered. "He may be my father, but he's also a really nice guy."

The call waiting signal beeped in Ali's ear. She glanced at the readout—Chris's cell phone. As soon as she saw the number, she felt guilty. She hadn't called her son—deliberately hadn't called him—when things started going bad. She had considered the mess to be her problem. With Chris starting a new job and a new life, she hadn't wanted to embroil him in her difficulties. But then, she hadn't much wanted Edie Larson and Dave Holman to be dragged into the situation, either.

Ali ended the call with Matt as soon as possible, but by then, Chris had left an irate voice mail message: "Mom. What the hell is going on out there? Call me."

"I knew you were busy," she said, once she had Chris on the phone. "I didn't want you to worry. How much have you heard?"

"I just got off the phone with Gramps, who talked to Grandma. I know Paul is dead. I know April's mother fell down a flight of stairs and could very well die, and that the cops think you're a suspect in both cases."

"That just about covers it then," Ali said as lightly as she could manage. "Sounds like you're completely up to date."

"Mother!" Chris exclaimed accusingly.

Chris hardly ever called her "Mother." It usually meant that the two of them were on the outs. And the reverse was true when Ali called him Christopher. This time she was the one who had crossed their invisible line.

"Tell me now," Chris ordered. "I want to hear it from you."

And so Ali did—she told him everything.

"I'm guessing April's mom is the one who came up with the idea of pushing for a postmortem divorce," Chris said when she finished.

"Either she did or her lawyer did," Ali said. "I'm not sure which."

"If anybody would know the ins and outs of divorce, Monique Ragsdale would probably be it," Chris said.

"What do you mean?"

"Monique's had several," Chris replied. "Divorces, that is. Scott Dumphey, one of the guys I used to play basketball with in college, is good friends with Jason Ragsdale, April's stepbrother. That's how I found out about Paul and April in the first place—through Scott."

The comment made it clear to Ali that there was a whole lot she didn't know about April Gaddis's family situation.

"April has a stepbrother?" Ali asked.

"'Had' is the operative word," Chris corrected. "Jason is a former stepbrother. From what I remember of the story, Jason's dad was a widower, an optometrist with a fairly decent nest egg, when April's mother arrived on the scene with April in tow. When Monique dumped the poor guy a couple of years later, his nest egg was a whole lot smaller."

Ali had no way of knowing if any of this information would prove useful or not. Nonetheless, she used a piece of hotel notepaper to jot down all the relevant names.

"What about April's dad?" Ali asked.

"What about him?" Chris returned. "I'm assuming he was several husbands ago."

That little tidbit of information made April's way of dealing with the world much more understandable. She had been raised by an often-married gold digger of a mother. That kind of background made it entirely reasonable for her to grow up thinking someone else's husband—anyone else's husband—was fair game. If that was how Monique had gotten ahead in the world, why wouldn't her daughter try doing the same thing? In that context, April's involvement with Paul Grayson must have seemed like business as usual.

"Anything else you can tell me about April?"

"Dropped out of college after only a semester or two," Chris replied. "According to Scott, she's not all that bright. At least he didn't think so."

Even with the door to April's room pulled shut, Ali wasn't prepared to comment on that either way.

"What's going to happen now?" Chris asked. "And

should I call in to work and have them get me a substitute teacher so I can drive over to help out?"

"No," Ali said. "Absolutely not. Mom's here. So's Dave Holman."

"He is? What's Dave doing there?"

"Grandma called him and he came."

"She called him, but she didn't call me."

Chris sounded understandably hurt.

"I'm sure she was thinking the same thing I was— that we didn't want to bother you or take you away from what you're doing."

"Thanks a lot," Chris said. "To both of you. Like mother like daughter, I guess, but I'm a grown-up now. I get to choose, remember?"

Ali would have said more, but call waiting buzzed again. The readout said Cedars-Sinai Medical Center. At the same time, her phone was telling her she was running out of battery power.

"Sorry, Chris," Ali told her son. "There's another call. I have to take it." She switched over.

"April Gaddis?" a male voice asked.

"No. April's in the other room, lying down."

"This is the contact number we were given, and it's about her mother. Can you put her on the line, please?"

The caller's voice sounded so distant, so impersonal, that Ali knew without hearing another word that the guy wasn't calling with good news.

"Just a moment," Ali said quickly. "She's resting, but I'll get her for you."

With the low-battery alarm still sounding, Ali hurried into April's darkened room. The young woman lay on her side, snoring softly. Ali shook her awake. "April," she said. "There's a call for you."

April took the phone. "Yes," she said. "What is it? Is my mother all right?

But of course Monique Ragsdale was anything but all right. She had died on the operating table, most likely as a result of the brain injury. With a slight whimper, April dropped the phone. As soon as it fell, Ali Reynolds knew she was now a suspect in two separate homicides.

Sobbing, April buried her face in the pillow. "Mom's gone," she wailed. "So's Paul. I'm all alone now. What's going to happen to me? What's going to happen to the baby?"

Ali reached down and patted April's shoulder. "I'm so sorry," she said. "But you'll be all right. We'll figure it out."

Then Ali picked up the phone, took it into the other room, plugged it into the charger, and called Victor Angeleri at home. "You need to know what's happened."

In the end, Ali stayed behind at the hotel for yet another meeting with Victor. Her mother and Dave were the ones who volunteered to take April back to the hospital to handle whatever paperwork needed signing. After several phone calls, Victor managed to locate Detectives Tim Hubbard and Rosalie Martin, the two L.A. homicide cops who were now in charge of the Monique Ragsdale investigation.

"Look," Victor said once he had Detective Hubbard on the phone. "I don't like the circus atmosphere any more than you do, and it's going to get a lot worse before it gets better. My client is willing to cooperate and give you a voluntary statement, but it needs to be done on our terms. I'd rather do it here at the hotel, where we have some control over the media. How about if you come to us?"

In the end, that's what happened—the detectives agreed to come there. For the next two hours, and with a tape recorder running, they went over the whole story again, in great detail. They wanted to know who was at the morning meeting at the house on Robert Lane. Both detectives seemed intrigued by the pre-funeral reading of Paul Grayson's will, and they seemed especially interested in the fact that Paul Grayson's murder had left Ali holding a bagful of monetary goodies.

"What was Ms. Gaddis's reaction to that?" Rosalie Martin wanted to know.

Ali shrugged. "What you'd expect. She was upset."

"What about her mother, Ms. Ragsdale?" Detective Hubbard asked. "Was she upset, too?"

"I'm sure she was worried about her daughter—and the baby," Ali told her.

"Which put the two of you on opposite sides of the fence."

Ali glanced in Victor's direction. He gave a slight shake of his head, and Ali said nothing more.

With the topic of the will pretty much exhausted, Hubbard moved on to other issues. The two cops seemed to have missed the Sumo Sudoku craze entirely and had to have the concept explained to them. When it came to the names of the players and the film crew, however, Ali wasn't able to offer much detail.

"What about workmen?" Detective Hubbard asked.

"Jesus Sanchez is the gardener," Ali said.

"What can you tell us about him?"

Ali shrugged. "Not much. He more or less came with the house. He was working there long before Paul and I bought the place. Most of the time he works alone, but today he had a crew working with him. I didn't know any of them."

Was this the time Ali should mention her near-encounter with the falling boulder, or would the cops see that as nothing more than a lame attempt on her part to deflect their suspicions away from her? She decided to let it go.

"What about the cook?" Detective Hubbard asked.

"I met her, but she's new. I don't know her name."

"What about address information or contact numbers for the two of them?"

"Jesus and the cook? I'm sure Paul had the information, probably in his office somewhere, but I don't. We were getting a divorce, remember?"

"We'll see what we can find," Hubbard said. "Now about the house. Does it have a security system?"

"Of course," Ali told him.

"But it wasn't alarming when you got there this afternoon and found Ms. Ragsdale at the bottom of the stairs?"

"No. The front door was half open but the alarm wasn't sounding. I assumed someone must have switched it off."

"Why would that be?"

"Maybe with so many people coming and going throughout the day, it was easier to turn it off."

"Isn't that unusual?"

"It would have been for me," Ali said. "But I'm not sure about how April runs the house."

"Your house," Hubbard added.

Ali didn't like it that Hubbard seemed so eager to come back to the idea that the house on Robert Lane ultimately belonged to Ali.

"April Gaddis is the one who's been living there most recently," Ali returned. "Maybe she's not all that worried about security."

"Maybe not," Hubbard agreed. "And no one else was there at the house when you arrived?"

"No one. Not the cook. Not the gardener."

"What time did you get there?"

"Four or so. I don't remember exactly."

"The nine-one-one call came in at four-fifteen."

"So around four."

"The people who were with you at the time you found Ms. Ragsdale were your mother and this friend, one Dave Holman."

"Yes," Ali said. "That's correct."

"And he's a police officer?"

Ali nodded. "Dave's a homicide detective with the Yavapai County Sheriff's Department in Sedona."

"I've heard about Sedona," Hubbard said. "The crystal place. So he drove all the way over here from there?"

"From Lake Havasu, actually," Ali replied. "He's divorced. He was there visiting his kids."

"When did he arrive?"

Ali was a little puzzled by this segue into questions about Dave Holman. "Early afternoon," she answered. "In time to have lunch."

"And he was with you most of the afternoon?"

"Yes."

All this time, Detective Rosalie Martin had been sitting back and letting her partner do most of the questioning. Now she leaned forward once more.

"You mentioned that you came and went from the hotel via the service elevator?"

"Yes," Ali said.

"Why was that?"

"Because the lobby was full of reporters. I wanted to avoid them if at all possible."

"Couldn't it also be because you didn't want to be observed, period?" Rosalie asked. "Not just by the reporters but by anyone?"

Her not-too-subtle implication was clear and Victor balked. "This interview is over," he announced. "My client has been more than cooperative. She's answered all your questions. If you want to know whether or not she left the hotel in the course of the afternoon, I suggest you avail yourselves of the hotel's security tapes. I'm sure those cover the service elevator as well as the public ones."

The cops left shortly thereafter. Victor turned to Ali. "Has anyone ever told you you're a hell of a lot of trouble?"

"Yes," she answered. "I'm pretty sure several people have mentioned it."

"By the way," Victor said. "My assistant did a LexisNexis search on you. We need to talk about the man you shot last March."

Having already been questioned by the cops for

more than an hour, Ali was surprised when Victor began grilling her as well.

"What about him? Ben Witherspoon was a vicious man who broke into my house and attacked me. I shot him, all right, but since he attacked me in my own home, the shooting was ruled self-defense, and I'd do it again in a minute."

"What about the lady who tried to force you off the highway? She's dead, too, isn't she?"

"Yes, but—"

"Do you happen to see a pattern here?" Victor asked.

"I do see a pattern," Ali said, her temper rising. "You seem to be giving me hell about all kinds of things that have nothing whatsoever to do with what's going on here. Why? Aren't you supposed to be my attorney?"

"I am your attorney. It's my job to look down the road, see what's coming in our direction, and do what I can to mitigate it. All those reporters down in the lobby—the ones who aren't getting a chance to interview you—are doing exactly the same thing I did. They're checking out every available bit of Ali Reynolds's history they can, including every archived posting on cutlooseblog.com. By the time you wake up tomorrow morning, regardless of whether or not you've been officially charged with a crime, you're going to be on trial in the media for everything you've ever said or done. They're going to turn you into this year's big story. You'll be cast as a former media elite who considers herself above the law and is probably getting away with murder."

"All I did was defend myself. Bringing up those old cases isn't fair."

"No, it's not," Victor agreed. "But that's how it's going to play out, especially if charges are brought in either one of these new cases."

"What about innocent until proven guilty?"

"Don't be naive, Ali," Victor said. "You know as well as I do, perception is everything, and the media are the ones who control that. Even if we prove you innocent in a court of law, dodging the criminal charge will only be the start of your problems. Next on the agenda will be a wrongful death suit where the burden of proof will be far less stringent. As Paul Grayson's primary heir, you'll make a very inviting target. Where's your gun, by the way?"

"My Glock? It's in the safe in Mom's and my room, but it's also legal. I have a valid license to carry."

"Valid or not, leave your gun in the safe," Victor advised. "If you end up being questioned again, you'll be way better off if the cops don't find a weapon on your person."

Before Ali could reply, the door opened and Dave Holman ushered April into the room. She looked ghastly. "I think she needs to lie down," Dave said.

As Ali rose to relieve Dave of his charge, Victor gathered his briefcase and stood as well. "I'll be going then," he said. "Hopefully for the last time today."

Ali led April into the other room, where she flopped down onto the bed without even stripping off her clothes. "Are you all right?" Ali asked.

"I'm tired," April said. "My back hurts. I need some sleep."

Ali left her there and returned to the other room, closing the door behind her. She found Dave standing by the window. "I don't think your attorney likes me," Dave said.

"That's fair enough," Ali said, "since I'm not so sure I like him very much at the moment, either. How was it?"

"The hospital?" Dave shook his head. "Not a good scene," he replied. "I felt sorry for April. It's a lot for someone her age to handle."

Ali nodded and looked around the suite, realizing for the first time that Edie hadn't returned with Dave. "What about Mom?" she asked.

"Said she was dead on her feet," Dave replied. "Told me to tell you she was going to bed and not to worry about waking her when you come in. She said she'll take out her hearing aids and won't hear a thing."

"Why wouldn't she be tired?" Ali returned. "I'm sure she got up at the usual time this morning and drove all the way here. Now it's way past her bedtime."

"What about your bedtime?" Dave asked. "And what about dinner? Did you have anything to eat?"

"Not since lunch."

"I'll take you to dinner then."

"What about the reporters?"

Dave grinned. "Don't worry. I'm not stupid. I've learned the drill. You call the bellman, go up and down in the service elevator, and hand over the tip. How do you think I got April in and out without being seen? And then there's my secret transportation device."

"What's that?"

"I'm sure the reporters have spotters keeping an eye on your Cayenne. And I don't doubt there was a huge flap when Victor took off in that enormous Lincoln of his. But it turns out nobody pays the least bit of attention to a beat-out Nissan Sentra. It's right up there with one of Harry Potter's invisibility cloaks."

Ali was genuinely surprised. In the months since she'd stopped working, she had returned to her long-neglected habit of reading for pleasure. She had allowed herself the guilty indulgence of reading the entire Harry Potter series and had enjoyed it far more than she had expected.

"You read Harry Potter?" she asked.

Dave rolled his eyes. "I've got kids, don't I? Now, are you coming to dinner or not?"

"Where are you taking me?"

"Somewhere no one will expect to find you," he said. "Denny's. And don't give me any grief about it. After forking over a fortune in tips this afternoon, it's the best I can do."

"Are you kidding?" Ali asked. "If you're offering a Grand Slam, I'm there."

{ CHAPTER 10 }

In the months Ali had been back home in Sedona, she had become reacquainted with the small-town intimacy of the Sugar Loaf Café. Now she found herself disappearing in the bustling anonymity of a corporate-run restaurant. The colorful, multipage plastic menus were the same everywhere. So was the food. The meal Ali ordered was good, but it didn't come close to measuring up to one of Bob Larson's.

"Victor thinks you should leave," Ali told Dave over dinner. "You and Mom both. He's afraid that having you poking around will somehow 'muddy the waters.'"

"Tough," Dave Holman replied. "I don't like Victor. Victor doesn't like me. That makes us even. I have three weeks of vacation coming. I called the office this afternoon and told Sheriff Maxwell I'm taking 'em. I'm here for the duration. And if things get settled sooner than that, I'll camp out over at Lake Havasu and visit with my kids."

"How are they doing?" Ali asked.

While Dave had been off serving in Iraq with his reserve unit, Roxanne, his now-former wife, had taken up with a sleazy time-share salesman. Months earlier, when the new husband had been transferred to Lake Havasu, Roxanne had moved, taking Dave's kids with her. He had been devastated.

"Medium," Dave replied glumly. "Gary, the cretin, lost his job. Got caught in some kind of corporate hanky-panky. Roxie didn't tell me any of the gory details, and I'm probably better off not knowing. The thing is, Gary is currently unemployed, and they may end up having to move again. I'm not sure where—Vegas, maybe. The kids are sick about it. So am I."

"Have you thought about taking Roxie back to court and trying to get custody?" Ali asked.

Dave shook his head. "Are you kidding? I'm a man. I've got about as much chance of winning a custody fight as I do of winning at Powerball. And since I never buy a lotto ticket, that's not likely to happen. But let's not talk about that. Let's talk about you."

"What about me?"

"This is serious, Ali. Really serious."

"Victor has already pointed that out," Ali responded. "Several different times. And it could be serious for you, too. Earlier the LAPD cops were asking a lot of questions about you. So was Victor, for that matter."

"Screw Victor," Dave said. "But it makes sense. If the cops are looking for you to have an accomplice, then I could be a likely subject. Who better than a renegade homicide detective to figure out a way to cover up a murder?"

"So what do we do?" Ali asked.

"We fight back."

"But you can't do that, can you? You're a cop."

He smiled grimly. "You'd be surprised at what I can do. What did you tell the two homicide dicks?"

"I told them exactly what happened, that you and Mom and I were all together at the hotel this afternoon, right up until we went over to the house and found Monique at the bottom of the staircase. I got the impression that they were going to go check out the hotel's security tapes to see whether or not I was telling the truth about my comings and goings."

"Did they tell you what time Monique took her header?" Dave asked.

"No. Why?"

"Because she may have been on the floor for a long time before we found her. If she fell before I got to the hotel, we could still have a problem on that score."

"Is there any way to find out?" Ali asked.

"Officially, no," Dave replied. "Unofficially, maybe. I'm assuming they asked you who all was at the house today."

Ali nodded.

"You'd better tell me, too, then," he said. "Give me the whole list. As far as I'm concerned, it's time we started running our own parallel investigation."

"But—" Ali began.

"Victor Angeleri is looking out for you," Dave said, "but the man is being paid good money to look out for you. Nobody's paying my freight. I'm the one who has to look out for me. If you don't want to have anything to do with this, fine. I'll do it on my own."

"What do you need exactly?"

"I need you to tell me whatever you told them. In detail."

Knowing she had been leaving April's room for the night, Ali had dragged her computer along with her when she headed out. Now, at Ali's request, Dave went out to his Nissan and retrieved Ali's laptop. For the next hour or so, Ali told the story one more time, using her air-card network to pluck appropriate telephone numbers and addresses off the Internet. Dave's method was far more low-tech. He jotted his notes expertly on a series of paper napkins, including the part about her close encounter with the boulder.

"You're sure it was an accident?" Dave wanted to know.

"I think it was an accident," Ali told him. "It *looked* like an accident, but with everything else that's gone on . . ."

"We'd better check it out," Dave said.

When they finally finished the grueling process, Ali was a rag. "I've got to go back to the hotel," she said. "It's time."

By then it was late enough and the lobby deserted enough that Ali risked venturing in through the front door. Upstairs, walking toward her room on what was posted as a nonsmoking floor, she was surprised to find the corridor reeking of cigarette smoke. She was tempted to call back down to the lobby to complain, but then she thought better of it. The last thing April or Edie needed was someone from hotel security pounding on doors and waking everybody up.

Inside the room, Ali found that her mother hadn't bothered to close the blackout curtains. Even without turning on a light, there was plenty of illumination for Ali to find her way around the room. Her mother was sound asleep, clinging to the far side of the single king-sized bed. Ali undressed and climbed in on the other side. By the time her head hit the pillow, she was asleep. She awakened to the click of the door lock and the smell of coffee as Edie let herself back into the room. A glance at the clock told Ali it was past seven.

"Sorry to wake you," her mother apologized. "I've been up since four, and I finally couldn't stand it anymore. I had to go downstairs to get some coffee and the newspapers."

She unloaded two paper cups and a stack of newspapers onto the coffee table while Ali got up and staggered into the bathroom.

"You must have gotten home late," Edie observed over the top of a newspaper when Ali emerged.